JEANNE WILLIAMS

Hendrick-Long Publishing Co.
Dallas, Texas

Library of Congress Cataloging-in-Publication Data

Williams, Jeanne
New medicine / Jeanne Williams.
p. cm.
Summary: When his tribe is forced to go to Fort Sill Reservation, the son of a Comanche chieftain debates whether to continue his resistance or to adapt to the white man's ways.
ISBN 0-937460-90-7 (hardback). — ISBN 0-937460-93-1 (pbk.)
1. Comanche Indians—Juvenile fiction. [1. Comanche Indians—Fiction. 2. Indians of North America—Fiction.] I. Title.
PZ7.W66624Ne 1993
[Fic]—dc20 93-37756
CIP
AC

Design and Production: Dianne J. Borneman, Shadow Canyon Graphics, Evergreen, Colorado
Maps and Cover Illustration copyright © 1994 by Michael Taylor, Prescott, Arizona

Printed in the United States of America

Hendrick-Long Publishing Company
Dallas, Texas 75225-1123

NEW • MEDICINE

For

David and Jason

May your Medicine be powerful and good

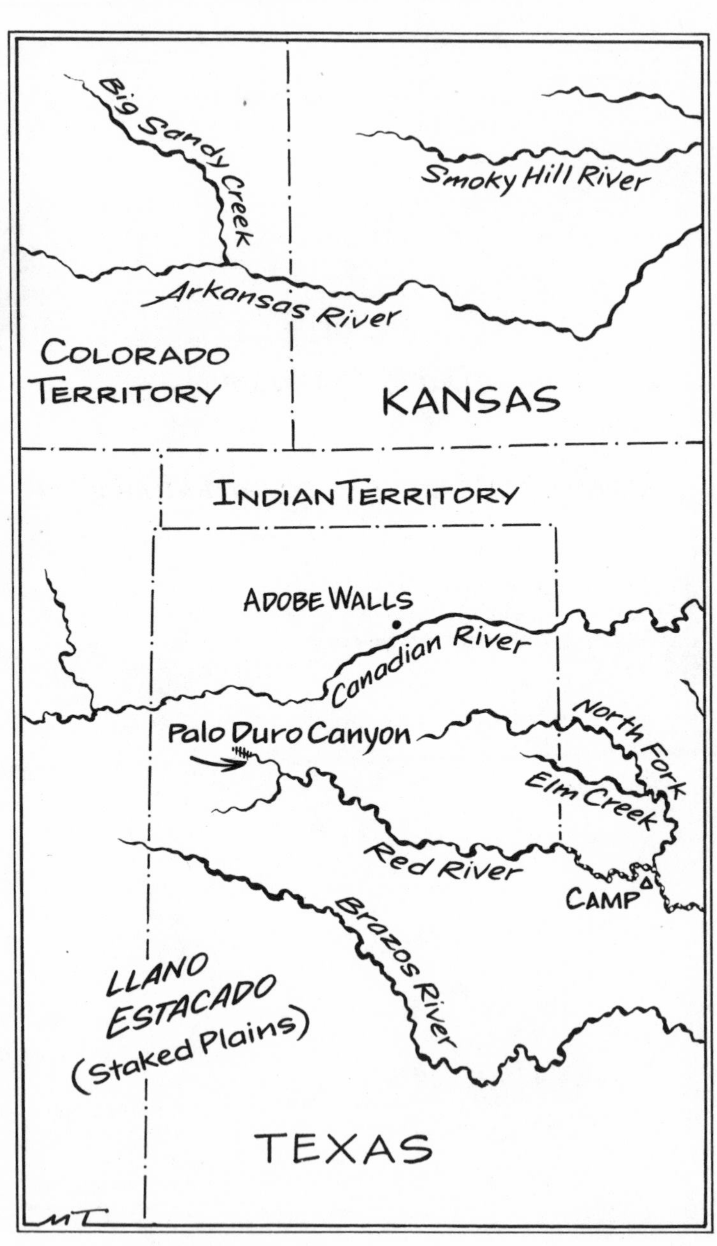
Big Sandy Creek
Smoky Hill River
Arkansas River
COLORADO
TERRITORY
KANSAS
INDIAN TERRITORY
ADOBE WALLS
Canadian River
Palo Duro Canyon
North Fork
Elm Creek
Red River
CAMP
Brazos River
LLANO
ESTACADO
(Staked Plains)
TEXAS
MT

Smoky Hill River
Arkansas River
KANSAS
INDIAN TERRITORY
Wichita Mountains
Canadian River
Ft. Sill
Washita River
Cache Creek
Red River
TEXAS
Brazos River
N

Chapter One

This was the Comanche's first Sun Dance lodge, but they had taken great care to make it right, for the power they sought in this dance must be much greater, much stronger, than any medicine ever made before. Walker stood gripping his bow and best arrow, the one with eagle feathers and a painted groove. His offering to the spirits was fastened to the arrow.

He looked up to the great center pole of the lodge, from which hung the stuffed body of a young buffalo bull killed by one arrow. Fine clothes, ornaments, robes, beaded work, and beautifully tanned hides—presents of all kinds—were tied to the center pole. Streamers ran from it to each of the twelve upright posts circling it.

The spaces between these were filled in with brush except for an opening to the east. After all the Comanche bands had gathered where Elm Creek joined the Red River, it had taken four days to make the lodge because everything had to be done just right in order to get the

powerful medicine that the people had to have, medicine to shove the white men back from the hunting grounds.

The Comanche had no sacred doll like the Kiowa or special Sun Dance Priest with a Sun Dance medicine bundle like the Cheyenne, but the Comanche had watched neighboring tribes give the dance till they knew exactly how it must be done, even to having the center pole cut by a respected woman, preferably a captive in case the power killed her, and the pole hoisted into place after three false starts.

All was done and done well. For the first time ever all Comanche bands had come together, called by Isatai the Prophet. Walker would never forget how, on the fourth evening, a crier had gone through the camp calling the people to gather before their lodges.

Each band, doing its favorite dance, had moved toward the dance lodge in the center of the huge encampment, and there they had danced, all Comanche together, united for the first time—Yap Eaters from the north, Antelope from the Staked Plain, Buffalo Eaters, whose favored range was the Canadian River Valley, and Liver Eaters and Wanderers from their central prairies along the Red River and the Brazos.

Only the Wasps had gone back to their timbered home below the Brazos when they learned the purpose of the Sun Dance. For many years they had lived closer to Caddo, Wichita, and whites than they had lived near other Comanche. Let them go!

Kiowa who had been camped a little north would take their place, and the Cheyenne were making medicine, too. Walker had never seen so many warriors. There were even some Apache and Arapaho.

Chapter One

Now as Walker stood inside the lodge, the old men sitting around the giant drum south of the entrance began to thump with their sticks and rattles. Painted dancers came out from behind the screen. Walker could smell the heavy, stinging scent of sage from the beds where the dancers rested when not dancing.

First Son, Walker's older brother, made little jumps in time to the drumbeats, blowing on the eagle-bone whistle between his teeth. None of the dancers had eaten or drunk since the dance began four days ago. First Son looked worn out, in spite of his bright paint, but soon his thirst and hunger should be turning into power.

Tonight there would be a feast, but the dancers would only feel like drinking some broth before sinking into sleep. Power was hard to get, but a warrior must have it in order to do great things.

Walker drew a long deep breath. He had gone on the buffalo hunt last fall but was just learning to be a warrior. More than anything, he wanted to go on this huge war party, help drive away the whites who were crowding into the lands promised by treaty to the Indians. But this would be a raid for warriors, the best ones, and Walker was young, not quite fifteen.

Worse, nothing within Walker had yet told him to go on a medicine quest. No bird or beast had come to him in a vision and given him its power.

Several times in the past year Walker had almost gone anyway, picked some spot where other men had found visions. Twice he had gone so far as to collect his pipe, tobacco, and blanket, but both times his heart had told him the spirits were not ready.

New Medicine

Medicine could not be won by force. A youth could fast and pray, join in the Sun Dance, seek, reach, long and hunger for power; but if the spirits were not willing, nothing brought medicine.

Walker wanted power so much that he was afraid to seek it till his heart was drawn by some spirit. He was determined that when he did go on his quest, he would not come back unblessed. He would stay till he starved or received a sign. That was dangerous, to set one's will hard and try to force the spirits. Walker knew that, but it was how he felt. All he could do was show respect by waiting as long as he could to seek his medicine.

First Son, of course, had met a vision the first time he went out. It must have been very strong power, the kind the spirit must have warned him not to talk about, but everyone knew First Son had got medicine from the way he acted when he came home.

The spirit who gave power told how to take care of it, what you must do and could not do. Some kinds of medicine had so many rules and were so hard to keep that the owners had taken the medicine back to the place where they got it, thanked the spirit, and respectfully given back the power. The stronger medicine was, the harder it was to live with.

A man without medicine was like a man without coups, poor and respected by no one. The more dangerous his medicine was, the higher was his honor. Walker hoped that if he went on this war party he could show the spirits that he was brave so that one would surely bless him.

That was why he had tied his greatest treasure, a pair of silver earrings his father, Spring Bull, had fastened to his cradle, on this arrow which he now aimed toward

Chapter One

the center pole and let fly with just enough force to stick next to the streamers by the buffalo.

The earrings gleamed brightly. Walker swallowed. His father had not given him many presents. It had been hard to part with the birth gift. But if the spirits saw and understood—if they moved Spring Bull to let him go on the raid—it would be worth all Walker had.

Walker was not overlooking earthly help, either. After the Sun Dance ended, he would ask First Son to speak to their father. First Son was kind and helped Walker, although things had always been easy for First Son as the favored child of a great chief. Without even seeming to try, First Son was best at nearly everything. He had taught Walker to hunt and had looked after him during the big buffalo hunt last year.

First Son was all that Walker longed to be.

A breeze, wonderfully cooling, struck Walker as he came out of the lodge, and he realized how he had been sweating in the lodge. As he made his way to his mother's tipi, he passed two Kiowa youths of about his age, glittering with silver ornaments. The Kiowa loved silver and used all they could get.

The boy wearing the most silver and a handsome quiver of cougar skin had his back to Walker, the center part of his long black hair painted vermilion. He was laughing.

"One would think as long as the Comanche have watched us do this dance they would have learned something! What good is the dance without a taime doll?"

Walker halted, his blood running thick and hot. Such talk might hurt the medicine! You had to be polite to guests, but guests should be polite, too.

This dance wasn't just for power to help Comanches, but to gain medicine for all the Indians! Yet this frippish, dressed-up Kiowa who probably hadn't even killed a buffalo stood around finding fault! Walker got control of his voice, then spoke.

"Friend."

The Kiowa whirled, startled. He was darker than Walker, dark even for a Kiowa, a good-looking boy if he had not been so skinny.

"Friend," went on Walker. "Do you have good dances since the Ute took two of your medicine dolls?" This had happened several years ago and was a great shame to the Kiowa.

The boy stared at Walker, brows pulled together. Walker smiled mockingly. He couldn't start trouble, but—

"It is good to see young men of different tribes talking together." Both boys swung toward the amiable deep voice. "That is how to understand things."

Recognizing the young chief with strange blue eyes, Walker felt his smile dry on his lips, and inside, too. Quanah, son of a captive white woman, was not a warrior to be laughed at behind his face. Spring Bull said that Quanah would become the greatest of all living Comanche chiefs, though there were many, even in Quanah's own Antelope, or Quohada, band, with much more experience.

"There are different ways to do the same thing, and one way may be as good as another and suit some people better." Quanah smiled at the Kiowa boys. "You have camp police, and they help run your buffalo hunts. We Comanche don't, but we get buffalo all the same. There are many ways to hold the Sun Dance! The Ponca and Sioux torture themselves—drive skewers through their

Chapter One

flesh, or hang themselves from the lodge poles, or chop off their fingers."

"We don't do that!" said the Kiowa boy. "That is crazy!"

"Still, it is the Sioux and Ponca way. And then the Crow only do the dance when a warrior wants revenge for the death of someone close to him." Quanah paused, seeming to cast about for other examples. "Some Indians eat dogs, but to other tribes they are tabu. You Kiowa won't eat bear, but Comanche do and are not harmed. It is all right to have different ways. The important thing is for us to come together in this dance, praying, willing one thing, making great medicine to save all of our peoples. I believe Isatai has the strongest power ever given—and not just because he can belch out cartridges ."

Quanah moved off with a sure, proud step. The boys looked at each other sheepishly, and Walker felt like hanging his head. Quanah meant that they must remember what they shared and not make fun of the other tribe's customs.

It was like medicine. Each man's had its own strength and its own rules, and it was dangerous to make fun of it. Walker smiled hesitantly at the Kiowa boys.

"We all have bows. Let's see if we can find some fresh meat!"

"Good!" said the thin, handsome boy.

His friend said he must go visit an uncle, so Walker and the boy, who gave his name as Bright Mirror, went out together.

Bright Mirror first sighted the deer, but Walker brought it down after the Kiowa's arrow missed. They reclaimed their arrows and shared the raw liver of the deer, deliciously flavored with its own gall, before packing the carcass home to Walker's mother.

Good Hands was outside the lodge, playing with a neighbor's child. She smiled at Walker and said to Bright Mirror, "Come in, friend. That is a fat, tender-looking deer you hunters have brought!"

The boys followed her inside. Bright Mirror looked around admiringly.

"This is the best tipi I have seen!" he told Good Hands.

She only made a modest clucking sound with her tongue, but Walker said proudly, "My mother is such a good tipi-maker, that other women bring her many presents so that she will help them make theirs. She stays busy all the time!"

"It is good to be busy," said Good Hands. "Now I must be busy at cooking the fine deer. Are you hungry?"

"We had liver," Walker said.

Good Hands straightened from rummaging in a leather bag. "Well, take these anyway," she said laughingly, giving each boy a handful of pumpkin seeds.

They thanked her and wandered back to watch the bustle around the Sun Dance lodge. So many warriors—so many strong brave men! Surely with the help of the Sun Dance medicine they could get rid of these whites who were creeping over the free lands like lice in a greasy blanket.

"What is it with this Isatai?" Bright Mirror asked. "Does he have great power, or is it only that his stomach burns because white men killed his uncle?"

"Do you remember that comet last year?" asked Walker. "Isatai said it would vanish after five days and leave a summer-long drought. It was as he said."

Chapter One

The Kiowa nodded, and the silver and bright yarn woven into his braids danced. "That is strong medicine!"

Stronger even than the medicine of Spring Bull, who belonged to the Eagle Shields as well as having great power from a vision. Spring Bull had enough medicine to give several sons a respectable portion, but his best power would go to First Son.

First Son had lived in his own good tipi since he was fourteen and had a valuable war-horse. Spring Bull had three wives, but First Son was the child of his first and favorite wife.

Spring Bull was good to Walker, but everyone knew First Son stood high above everything else in Spring Bull's heart. It would never have occurred to Walker to expect his own tipi because First Son had one. Walker knew that he would live in his mother's lodge until he married, which was the usual practice. Spring Bull had even taken First Son on raids and trained him, though most men sent their sons to learn from other warriors.

Sometimes Walker's heart felt shadowed when his father looked past him to First Son. It was like being a young tree trying to grow near a stronger-rooted older one which had tapped the water and taken most of the sunlight.

Still, Walker would rather have been the least-favored son of Spring Bull than the best-loved child of any other chief. And First Son was generous, swift to help, all that Walker yearned to be.

When the dance was over, Walker would ask him to speak to Spring Bull, persuade the chief to let Walker go on the raid. At twilight Bright Mirror went home, but Walker did not move till the dancers came out of the lodge.

Though all looked ready to drop with exhaustion, most of the warriors looked quietly jubilant. First Son did not. His face was haggard, and his eyes held feverish brightness. Still, he managed a smile as Walker hurried to him.

"Well, younger brother, was it a good Sun Dance?"

"It looked very strong," Walker said. "Brother, will you ask our father to let me go on the war party?"

"You are young—"

"Brother, it is the most important raid there will ever be! Perhaps I can win medicine! Please, brother, speak to our father for me."

First Son gave Walker a strange, almost haunted look. "Younger brother, it would be better for you not to go."

Walker bit his lip, turned almost angrily away. "Then I shall go alone! I will follow the war party and join the battle by myself."

The strong, lean hand of First Son fell on his shoulder. "I will ask our father, then."

They had reached the lodge of First Son's mother, who came out with a bowl of rich broth for her son. She wore a fringed collar with Spring Bull's many war honors, but though she moved with the pride and assurance of a great chief's favored wife, there was fear in her eyes as she looked at First Son, for the young man refused the broth, though he had fasted four days.

Fear gripped Walker, too, and heaviness, for as First Son went into the tipi, he seemed suddenly a shadow, not a strong young warrior who had just danced for power.

Chapter Two

Drums and criers summoned all warriors, Comanche, Kiowa, Cheyenne, and Arapaho, to the council. Walker, with Bright Mirror and the other boys, watched and listened from a respectful distance as the mightiest chiefs of the plains met to decide what they should do about the white men.

Quanah presided, though he was not the best known of the Comanche. He took the pipe and sent a puff to each of the four winds before passing it around the circle.

Stone Calf of the Cheyenne spoke of Sand Creek, the merciless killing of women and children by Chivington, then reminded the council of Custer's attack on a peaceful encampment along the Washita a few years past.

"We do not like bacon and flour," he concluded. "Our women do not like to make white man's bread. We are hunters. We like to eat buffalo meat!"

Rising next, Lone Wolf spoke for the Kiowa, and all the people knew the truth of his words. "White men break all their promises. They are building railroads across our lands. The Wichita and Caddo believed the whites and obeyed them, moving onto reservations. Look at them! Beggars, sick, going downhill each day! Isatai is a great prophet. Let us hear him and follow!"

When Isatai rose, there was silence louder than war cries. The young man wore a breech-cloth, moccasins, and a red sash. Bracelets of silver sparkled on his arms. Snake rattles hung from his ears, a red-tipped hawk feather adorned his hair, and he wore a small wolfskin medicine bag around his neck.

He fanned the council fire with a fan of eagle feathers so that the smoke curled around him as he appealed to the Great Spirit for aid. Then he spoke to the assembly in a ringing, confident voice that made Walker's blood leap.

"Brothers, chiefs, warriors! I have been to the spirit world to ask for help against the white men. The Great Spirit gave me bulletproof paint for you. He has promised to let us attack and vanquish the buffalo skinners' post at Adobe Walls. We will not lose a man, we shall triumph without firing a shot! Look! I have brought medicine arrows for you!"

He gave the arrows out to the warriors and made a great howling, like a wolf.

The Kiowa and Cheyenne promised to ride on the war party. The council ended with a feast. Everyone was laughing and boasting, eager to ride against the white men, eager to take back their ancient hunting grounds. Some Comanche warriors made a mock charge into the Cheyenne camp, and the Cheyenne made a counterraid.

Warriors from all the tribes danced about the campfire. Isatai controlled the wind and lightning! He had

Chapter Two

talked with the Great Spirit! The white men would be killed in their sleep, all of them, and that would warn the other hunters away!

Tomorrow—tomorrow morning—the warriors would start for Adobe Walls!

Walker and Bright Mirror watched the dancing for a while, eager for the day when they too would be warriors, chanting of past glories and looking to new ones.

"Are you going tomorrow?" Bright Mirror asked, as they drifted toward their lodges.

"My brother has promised to ask our father," Walker said. "Father has never refused First Son anything." He laughed a little bitterly, not at his favored brother, but because things were as they were, because his own pleading would never move Spring Bull. "I shall go."

"Then we can ride together," Bright Mirror said. "It will be a great day, a great raid!" He turned to his own lodge while Walker moved on to pause by First Son's, burning to know if Spring Bull had given consent, yet unwilling to disturb First Son, who had looked so strange and exhausted.

"Younger brother?" came First Son's voice.

"Yes," said Walker, heart thudding.

"Come in."

Walker entered, made out the form of his brother on the bed of fine robes. Always, without asking or even seeming to want it, First Son had the best of all things. He did not raise himself now, but his voice was kind and stronger than it had been.

"I have talked to our father. He says you may go. Now, Walker, you must ride with care and luck, or I shall be to blame."

"Isatai says we will kill the whites without losing a man of our own."

"I hope he is right," said First Son, a heaviness in his voice. "He has talked with the Great Spirit. I have not."

Walker felt impatient with First Son's mood. If First Son were not renowned for bravery, such muttering would give him the name of coward, and at the least, it was not talk for the night before a great war party.

"Thank you, older brother," he said and went to his mother's lodge.

Grass, high and thick from spring rains, sloped yellow as wind struck it and whispered back soft rose, rippling gently through all the in-between shadings. How it would fatten buffalo! And how buffalo would fatten Comanche, Kiowa, Cheyenne—Arapaho, too, Walker amended, looking at the spreading ranks of warriors from all the tribes as they rode westward that morning. Walker in his high, excited spirits was willing to include the Caddo and Wichita in his hopes for good hunting if they could leave their corn patches long enough. They must not really be Indians! They had always farmed, even before the whites tried to make all the Indians settle on little breadths of earth, scratch the soil to bring forth grain.

Corn was good. Sometimes Comanche traded with the Wichita for it. But meat was better, and buffalo was best.

Walker frowned in spite of his exhileration. He had seen no large herds this spring, and neither had anyone else. Usually, at this time of year, in this wide plains country, one saw vast herds that stretched as far as the eye

Chapter Two

could see. Walker gazed back east, toward Fort Sill, where the reservation Indians had drawn only half rations that spring and had been forced to eat their mules and horses. That was what happened to those who believed white men!

Far better to travel hard between water holes here on the Staked Plains, better to range free under the cruelest circumstances than be fed and penned. As long as he could remember, Walker had followed with his people from Mexico through Texas to the Arkansas, over the soft grassy plains through the Staked Plains and east of the mountains till one came to the high mountain country of the Utes. Indian country, all of it, with no people better known or more respected than the Comanche.

It was fitting that the Comanche should lead the tribes against the hunters who were ruining the land.

Bright Mirror rode close to Walker and wrinkled his nostrils. "I smell something bad!"

The odor filled Walker's nose as the breeze shifted. He, Bright Mirror, and several of the other boys who had begged leave to come were riding at the rear with the extra horses and could not see everything, but they heard the angry cry of First Son, who had been scouting ahead of the main party.

"Buffalo! Rotting—wasted for their hides!"

On top of a rise, Walker reined in his horse and stared, at first unable to believe, then sick, with anger all the time burning hotter in his belly.

On a hillside opposite, skinned carcasses lay thick as tree trunks felled by a tornado, fifty or sixty in a pile, where the hunters had slaughtered them. Coyotes and birds feasted; they would have plenty for days.

New Medicine

After its first stunned fury, the war party rode past the stinking heaps as fast as it could. Walker felt a humming, vile taste in his throat and mouth, forced it back. He knew that his people could kill buffalo just to savor a tongue, but waste was unusual, whereas the whites seldom used more than the hump and tongue, and often not even those, but took the hides and let the meat rot.

One hunter with a gun could kill more of the huge beasts in a day than a hunting party using bows would in a week.

Gray Owl, a friend of Spring Bull and a famous medicine man, was riding close enough for Walker to hear as he gave a harsh laugh and touched his scalping knife.

"I hope the hunters who killed that herd are at Adobe Walls. Whites are not really white, you know, but gray or pink, and their blood is red like anyone's."

Walker glimpsed the sagebrush-stem cap of Isatai. Scalps trailed from the young chief's bridle, and his pony gleamed with the wonderful magic paint that would protect it from bullets. Walker's heart lifted, and he rode as fast as his position allowed. They were beyond the evil, decaying smell—several hundred warriors of allied tribes following the prophet chief who had talked with the Great Spirit—and braves had been catching up, joining the party, all afternoon. Once past the slaughtered buffalo, spirits lifted, and even the war-horses seemed to step with gaiety and pride.

Still, it bothered Walker that First Son did not smile.

On the third evening the war party camped five or six miles from Adobe Walls. Bright Mirror went off to his Kiowa elders to paint himself, while Walker put his effort

Chapter Two

into painting his good little dun pony. He did not intend to paint himself until he was a proved warrior, but he saw First Son coming, painted with vermilion, black, and yellow, and admired the fierce effect. He carried his shield, a good one, laced around the edge and stuffed with pages from white men's books. Some shields had great medicine and were a lot of trouble, having to be kept away from the fat or water, but First Son's shield had no special power and could be used without much thought or precaution.

First Son walked around Walker's horse and nodded approval. Then he looked straight at Walker and said quietly, "Brother, if anything happens to me tomorrow, take my horse and use him. I do not want him killed over my grave."

Walker's flesh chilled. "Don't talk that way, older brother! You have medicine—"

"Come with me," said First Son.

They walked to a gully where camp sounds were muffled, and First Son began to undo the medicine bundle he always wore on raids. It was wrapped in a fine otter skin. Walker had often wondered, enviously, what strong power was in it.

"You must never tell anyone what I am going to show you," First Son said.

Walker drew back, full of dread. His voice stuck in his throat. "Don't show me your medicine!"

First Son spread out the otter hide. "Do you see?"

Walker peered. "It's too dark." He shivered.

This was bad. He wished First Son would not act like this.

"Feel," urged First Son. "Smell!"

He gripped Walker's reluctant fingers and made them touch all over the otter skin. "What is there, younger brother?"

"Tobacco. Pemmican. Flint—steel—"

First Son let him go. "Yes. They are all the power I have. Something to eat, something to smoke, a way to make fire."

"But—"

"You thought I had power?" First Son gave a short laugh. "Think. Did I ever say I had a vision, a medicine dream?"

Walker thought back, realized with wonder and alarm that First Son had never claimed to have medicine. He had looked so tired, staying in bed for several days, that everyone had been sure his medicine was very strong. It had never occurred to Spring Bull, of course, that his favorite son had not been blessed with a vision.

Groping, bewildered, Walker persisted. "But the Sun Dance—"

"I prayed and danced and fasted till I could not stand. All I saw was the stuffed buffalo seeming to bloat and fall on me. I have seen more than that when I stayed in the sun too long." First Son made a helpless gesture, and Walker felt a great rush of sympathy for this brother who had seemed, till this moment, so fortunate. "I do not know what is wrong. I cannot ask my friends. Maybe there is no more medicine. If there is, it is not for me."

"Be careful tomorrow," Walker urged. "Talk with our father as soon as we get back." Spring Bull had not come, wanting First Son to have the glory of this raid to himself. "Our father has the shield and lance and can give you his other medicine."

"He cannot give power if the spirit refuses."

Chapter Two

"Then why have you been lucky in all things?"

First Son laughed again, and it was not a good sound. "I have to be brave on raids because I have no help, nothing besides myself. And I—I had hoped some spirit might relent and give me medicine if I were brave enough."

"It will happen tomorrow," Walker insisted.

First Son spoke as if driven to voice his secret doubts to someone. "Walker, perhaps I should not tell you this, but I am not sure that Isatai has been to the sun."

"But—many chiefs have seen! You were there!"

"I was present when many said they saw him go to the sun and descend—but I did not see this!" First Son caught Walker's shoulder, gripping it till it pained. "Isatai said he would go above and told us to watch the sun. We all did—and you know how one cannot gaze long at that blazing. Then he told us to behold him, that he had returned. There he was!"

Walker shifted restively. "I do not understand—"

"We all saw black spots going into the sky. They were supposed to be Isatai." First Son's voice fell to a whisper. "But Walker, I looked at the sun other times and always saw the same spots. It is the blaze in the eye that causes them, not Isatai!"

Walker did not answer. His mind whirled. But his clearest thought was that First Son was sick in his mind. Everyone else believed Isatai. Quanah did!

First Son folded the bundle, fastened it about his neck, and straightened. "If you do not get my shield wet, it will last you a long time."

They walked back to camp in silence.

Walker scarcely slept that night, his excitement over the raid smothered by worry over First Son which would not ease however much Walker assured himself that the power would surely come to his brother next day, that it had only waited to come at the high moment when the Indians started to shove back the whites.

Why, Walker hoped to do great things himself in the morning! He pictured himself charging the hide hunters' stronghold, but always, at the high point of his dreams, he felt beneath his fingers the dead hide of the otter skin which held no medicine.

At daybreak, the warriors formed in a long line. Quanah and Big Bow led the Comanche, Stone Calf and White Shield were in charge of the Cheyenne, while Woman's Heart and Lone Wolf commanded the Kiowa.

Riding up from the river, the warriors formed a new line at the timber edge along Adobe Creek facing the sod and log structures of the outpost, which lay in a shallow valley ringed by hills. On one hill, to the right of the line of warriors, Isatai sat on his painted horse, wearing only his cap of sagebrush stems and painted yellow.

"Stay back and watch the horses," First Son told Walker and Bright Mirror, as he joined the Comanche ranks.

Isatai signaled.

The Mexican who had grown up among the Kiowa after being captured as a child on the Rio Grande blew his bugle, and the warriors charged in a thunder of hoofs.

Up they swept to the walls, surged around the buildings. But some of the whites were awake and armed, for Stone Calf's son fell from his mount, and a Comanche fell. There was a flurry around some wagons, shouts of triumph, and two new scalps were flourished.

Chapter Two

The warriors charged all over the place, getting behind stables and a great stack of buffalo hides, while from behind the walls the whites were shooting in force, sending a hail of bullets through which Quanah raced to pick up the wounded Comanche lying near a building. As the chief leaned low to swoop up the fallen man and bear him off, First Son rode past them as a cover, shouting to the white men, taunting them. Walker's heart leaped with pride and relief as First Son trotted back unscathed.

First Son must have medicine, whether he knew it or not! And the young brave acted like it as the day wore on, repeatedly sweeping past the walls, emptying his rifle. Walker followed him closely, but there was plenty to watch on this first raid, and Walker tried to see it all.

An old white man, followed by his dog, went out to a pump with a bucket. The men inside the post must be thirsty. Somehow, in spite of a barrage of shots from the Indians, the man filled his bucket and got back inside the walls, but his dog yelped and fell.

Quanah's horse gave a convulsive leap and collapsed. The chief scrambled behind a buffalo carcass for shelter. He seemed to be hurt but dodged to a plum thicket. First Son sped in to carry him to safety and brought Quanah back to the timber edge. The young chief was wounded between neck and shoulder blade, and his right arm was useless, at least for this day's fighting.

Warriors began blaming Isatai, asking him why his prophecy had failed. Stone Calf, grieved and angry at his son's death, came up to taunt the leader.

"If your medicine is so great, Isatai, get back my son's body!"

"This is not my fault," protested the naked young prophet. "One of you Cheyenne killed a skunk the day we left the Sun Dance camp. That was bad. It broke my medicine."

Whatever was the cause, the Indians were to have no swift victory. By the time the sun was slanting west, the warriors stayed near the rim of hills east and west of the buildings. Dead horses and oxen lay scattered around the buildings. The two men killed and scalped at the wagon were the only whites known certainly to be dead, but at least nine Indians had been killed, and several were wounded.

Disappointed about the raid's lack of success, some Indians stole up to the wagons and began taking whatever they could find. No one could get near the main buildings, for the whites seemed to have an inexhaustible supply of bullets. Too many horses and men painted with Isatai's magic paint lay dead for anyone to keep belief in his power.

Only First Son, who had never believed in the medicine anyway, grew bolder as his comrades lost faith. He shouted to Stone Calf, "I will bring back your son's body!" and rode toward the store.

It seemed he would reclaim the young Cheyenne's body. Swooping low for it, First Son suddenly threw back his arms and slipped to the ground like a folding banner. His horse sped on, but First Son lay still.

Walker cried out, started to kick his horse forward, but Bright Mirror caught his reins. "Don't go! You'll be killed!"

"I must get my brother!"

"Stay here, or your father will mourn two sons instead of one."

Chapter Two

Walker scarcely heard. He only saw that First Son was very quiet. Surely he was dead. But he could still be buried with honor if his body was saved. His spirit would not become an unhappy wanderer.

"Let me go," he ordered his friend.

"Wait," pleaded Bright Mirror. "Look, the sun is almost down. Wait till twilight tricks eyes, and I will go with you."

Walker paused. That was the safest, surest way to get back First Son's body. Then he saw a faint movement of his brother's arm.

Perhaps First Son lived!

Perhaps Walker would not have to go back to Spring Bull with terrible news.

Wrenching the reins away from Bright Mirror, Walker urged his pony forward. Slipping his foot into the plaited rawhide ring securely fastened in the horse's mane, Walker rode almost completely shielded by his horse.

Bullets whizzed by like angry hornets. One sent turf into Walker's face as he neared his brother. First Son's eyes were open. He reached up as Walker leaned over and gave himself a heave so that Walker could sweep him up.

Hanging on to his brother with all his strength, Walker heard the labored breathing and saw First Son's lips were blue, but it was not till they reached the refuge of the timber that Walker lowered his brother to the grass and saw how his intestines pushed in and out with his breath.

Quanah, right arm dangling useless, came up, and Gray Owl knelt by First Son, stuffing his entrails back inside, then burning the spines off a prickly pear and splitting the pad to press the open part on the wound.

"That is better," First Son panted. His paint was smeared, and drops of sweat stood on his forehead. He tried to smile at Walker, and his lashes fluttered. Walker remembered how proud First Son's mother was of his hair, always careful that he should have a good porcupine-hide brush and bright cloth for plaiting. Walker hurried to bring water from the creek.

When he came back with it, his brother was dead.

"I am sorry," Quanah said, rising.

"Let us beat the false prophet with our quirts," cried a Cheyenne named Hippy. "He should be dead instead of the warriors who believed him!"

"No one will ever follow him again," said another chief. "That is the worst punishment."

If Walker had not been grieving for his brother, he would have felt sorry for the young prophet who stood naked and deserted in his sage-stem cap. His magic-painted pony had been shot from under him. His prophecies had been proved wrong. There was no way at all for him to win back honor or the respect of warriors who now blamed or ignored him.

Gray Owl took Walker by the arm and led him a little distance from First Son. "Shall we find a good place to bury your brother?"

"I must take him home," Walker said numbly, still disbelieving. "How will I do that? Our father will hate me. I live and his favorite son is dead!"

"You did all you could," said Gray Owl. He sighed heavily, staring at his hands still marked with First Son's blood. "I would rather cure men than kill them!"

Bright Mirror had come up and said now, "I will ride with you to take your brother home."

Chapter Three

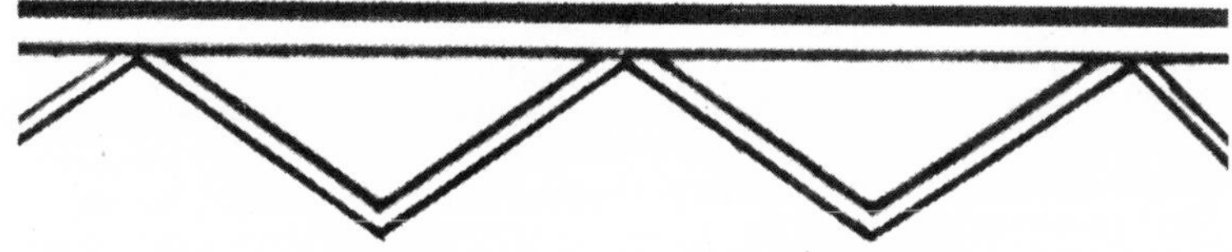

Walker wrapped First Son in a blanket. He did not want to travel at night with the body any more than necessary. Dead people did not like to be dead, especially when they were young like First Son, and this made them different from when they had been alive. It was good of Bright Mirror to accompany them.

Next morning, in the first gray dawn, Walker loaded his brother's body on his war-horse, the one he had given Walker, and started out. Bright Mirror rode alongside.

The other Indians had started to leave, scattering in small bands, though a few stayed around, hoping for another try at the post.

Walker and Bright Mirror camped in silence that night, both nervous and uneasily aware of the blanketed body which had to be kept near enough to be protected from carrion eaters.

Gray Owl and a few older warriors, friends of Spring Bull, caught up with them by noon and rode into camp with them, up to Spring Bull's lodge.

Spring Bull came out, the glad look on his face dimming. Then he saw the blanket-wrapped form on the war-horse. His step faltered. He stood quiet for a moment. When he moved forward, he was suddenly an old man.

"My son!"

He reached for the body, gathered it into his arms. He did not look at Walker but turned without a word and carried his dead son into the lodge.

Gray Owl looked at Walker. "Go to your mother and eat and rest. There is no more to do now."

"I must join my people," Bright Mirror said. "We will meet another time, friend."

"First you must eat," said Walker, rousing. "My mother will give you food to take on your journey."

Good Hands knew about First Son. She had hacked off her hair and cut her face in mourning, but she fed Walker and made a packet of food for Bright Mirror. When his friend was gone, Walker lay down to sleep.

He woke to the sounds of lament and wailing. Going out, he saw First Son's mother and hardly recognized her. She had chopped off two fingers and gashed her face. Surrounded by women, she sat by her lodge and wept. Spring Bull came out, holding a blanket painted yellow.

He fastened the blanket on First Son's war-horse, mounted his own pony. Walker went for his tired dun and followed. Spring Bull traveled north. There were some small buttes which would make good burial spots. Walker halted, glancing in question at his father, who looked at him for the first time.

"I am going to Medicine Bluff," said Spring Bull. "Perhaps the spirits there will give my son his life again."

Walker stared. Had Spring Bull gone mad?

Chapter Three

Spring Bull spoke harshly, almost as if he hated his living son. "You do not have to come." He started on, leading the burdened war-horse.

Walker followed, though he was afraid of First Son's spirit. It was not good to keep a body this way. Anything could happen!

A few days later, they came to the end of the mountains and reached the famous bluff near Cache Creek. Spring Bull unloaded the body, carried it to the rocks. He took no notice of Walker.

For three days Walker stayed near the bluff, snaring rabbits for food, hearing the faint sounds of Spring Bull's praying and singing to the spirits. Bright Mirror had meant to visit relations on the reservation not far away, and Walker was tempted to look for him, but he feared to leave the aging warrior across the creek who still beseeched the powers to give him back First Son.

On the fourth morning, Spring Bull returned, leading the war-horse, which still carried the yellow blanket.

"My son is not coming back. The medicine is no good here."

"Shall we bury him here, father?"

"He will not go beneath ground. He shall ride his pony as he always did, sleep in his tipi."

Walker's flesh crept as he got on his horse and went after Spring Bull. Had the great chief lost his mind? People would not like having bones around. They would probably camp at a safe distance from Spring Bull. Walker could not blame them. He had been First Son's brother, had loved and admired him, but it was not right or wise to keep company with skeletons!

When they came back to camp with the yellow-wrapped bones, only Spring Bull's great prestige and power kept people silent. He put First Son's bones in the young man's lodge and could be heard talking to them. Everybody said he was crazed and hoped he would get over it before some misfortune struck because of this madness.

Summer wore on, and still Spring Bull talked with his dead son, spent more time with the skeleton than with the living. Drifting Cheyenne said a war party had massacred a party of emigrants on the Smoky Hill River and taken captive four girls. A little later, other Cheyenne attacked a wagon train and burned a few white men, though the Cheyenne said Osage had done it in spite of that tribe's purported friendship with the whites.

The season became one long searing wind, a plague of grasshoppers across the plains, with all streams going dry except for the most unfailing water holes. Grass, burned by sun and devoured by grasshoppers, disappeared, and the Indians began to hunt the cause of their ill luck. Families began moving away from Spring Bull's group, but the chief seemed not to notice.

At last half a dozen of the best-known chiefs came to Spring Bull. Gray Owl spoke for them.

"Friend, let us bury your son."

"I cannot."

The chiefs looked with fear toward the lodge where First Son's remains lay. Walker, from his mother's tipi, listened with a pounding heart, praying that Gray Owl would reach Spring Bull's reason, but when Walker peered out, he saw the stubborn set of his father's shoulders as he looked slowly at his trusted old friends, two of

Chapter Three

them brothers-in-law, several of them members of his shield society.

"My son would be lonely underground," Spring Bull said. "I will take him, and we shall travel together, apart from the camp. Brothers-in-law, I give you my herds and horses. Care for my wives."

The men nodded. "We will do it."

Gray Owl lingered after the others had gone. "Spring Bull, old friend, your son is dead. Do not go after him till it is time!"

"Without him I have no life," said the mourning chief.

Gray Owl was a great medicine man and could heal many deep wounds, but he had no cure for this grief. He moved sorrowfully away. Spring Bull turned and went into First Son's lodge.

Walker looked at his mother, who was standing very still. She was not Spring Bull's favored wife, but that did not mean her feeling for her husband was not great.

"Mother," said Walker, torn two ways, "shall I stay here to hunt for you?"

"Go with your father," Good Hands answered. She was already preparing a bag of food, pemmican and jerked meat. "I can make tipis. And my brother will feed me."

Walker collected his belongings—extra moccasins, a fringed shirt and leggings for cold weather, arrows, bow, knife—and wrapped them in a good buffalo robe his mother brought.

Spring Bull was throwing himself away, as might be done with an old person who had no close relatives when food got scarce. It was a wild thing for a rich chief to do.

Perhaps the bones had already cast evil medicine on Spring Bull. Walker pushed the thought away with all his strength, though it was a bitter, hurtful thing to realize that he meant so little to his father, that without First Son life held no savor for Spring Bull.

Good Hands touched Walker's face. She was crying. "Be careful," she told him and gave him the packet of food.

Across the white and yellow soils of Texas, the gray earth of the Llano Estacado, or Staked Plain, the red ground of the Indian Territory, Walker followed the old chief, who led a war-horse burdened with a yellow-blanketed bundle. Winds from the whole south plains stung Walker's face, gaunted the horses.

Fortunately, they could camp most of the time. This gave Walker a chance to kill antelope, or even rabbit, turkey, or fish, while Spring Bull sat singing or talking to the bones.

Sometimes Walker almost hated his brother for having been so loved, but most of the time he simply endured, and it was worse than being solitary, for Spring Bull seldom spoke to him, though he carried on long conversations with his dead son.

One day they found an old buffalo with wolves tearing at him. Little remained of his legs except bones and tendons. His eyes were gouged out, yet he kept turning ponderously, trying to defend himself against the swift and ravening attackers.

Spring Bull got out an arrow, shot it into the side of the old buffalo, which toppled as if of its own weight. Walker retrieved the arrow and hacked off the best parts of the stringy meat.

Chapter Three

The summer blazed on, drying their bodies tough as the parched land. Sometimes they met hunting parties with little to show for their troubles; sometimes they came upon raiders. All the tribes were angry, welcoming any chance to strike at the whites.

Late in the season the wanderers came near their old camp, and Walker rode in to see his mother—also, though he would not clearly admit it, to prove to himself that there were other things in the world than a blanket of bones and an old man who sang to them.

"We are going to camp in the big canyon to the north," Good Hands told Walker. "If your father buries the dead one, come join us." She was thin, and Walker tried to refuse the parcel of food she pressed on him, but at last he took it and went after the gray old chief.

Walker had meant, that fall, to seek a vision, but now all he saw were blurrings of the merciless sun and here and there, too often, skinned and rotting piles of buffalo. Once they rode past Adobe Walls.

The post was abandoned, but a dozen Indian skulls grinned from the fence posts, staring with empty sockets across the plains. Spring Bull halted. Sudden rage seemed to catch him. He unsheathed his rifle, loaded, and fired at the nearest post.

Almost as if signaled, hunters came over the hill, white men, with their fast guns. Walker and Spring Bull made for the nearest cover, a buffalo wallow. Crouching behind its bank, they shot at their attackers, Spring Bull with his rifle, Walker with arrows.

The hunters were riding down. Spring Bull was singing, not to the bones this time but to earth and moon and sun, the things that remained though men died.

He had been a great chief; he had lived. But Walker felt despairing that he himself should die here with a demented old man and a skeleton. The hunters would take their scalps so that even their souls would wander! When Spring Bull spoke, it took Walker a moment to understand that his father called to him.

"My son! You have been faithful. The spirits have told me you will have much medicine, a different, new kind. You must keep a strong heart and help our people."

"Father—"

Spring Bull looked almost young again. His face was eager as he mounted. "Don't mourn for me with cuttings," he said, smiling down at Walker. "I am happy! I can save one son while going to the other!"

He gave a shout and rode forward, straight for the hunters. He toppled one of them before he fell. The whites either had not seen Walker or feared ambush, for they rode on, not even stopping to mutilate Spring Bull's body. When they had gone over the hills, Walker went to his father.

Walker dug a shallow cavern in a hill facing east, placed Spring Bull in it with his weapons and the yellow blanket still holding First Son's bones. Then Walker led the chief's horse over, a once splendid animal, old now and exhausted from the summer's hard travels. It stood quietly.

Walker cut its throat. It went down without a sound, joining its master. Walker cut off his own hair, started to chop off a finger, then hesitated.

Why maim himself? He had done all the service he could to Spring Bull while his father lived, and in the days ahead he would need all his fingers, all his strength.

Chapter Three

A few months ago he would have been afraid to camp alone near the dead, but following the bones had hardened him. He camped on the creek that night and next morning, leading First Son's war-horse, started east to find his people.

Chapter Four

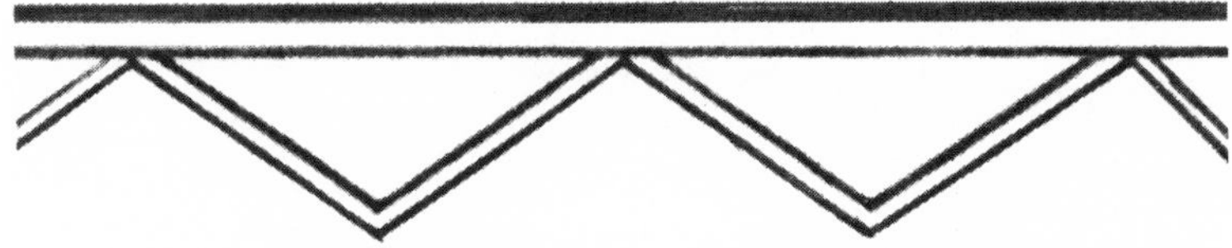

A cruel summer and a hard fall. Walker traveled in thunderstorms which even at night lit the plains with arrows and tremors of lightning, showing grass beat flat by the pelting rain. Once when he lay down in exhaustion, he woke to find tarantulas swarming over him, hunting an island shelter from the accumulating rainwater. Walker jumped up, brushing them off him, and rode again, though he was weak with hunger and the need for rest.

He wanted more than anything to get back to his people, to enter Good Hands' lodge and sleep in a peace and comfort he had not known since the Sun Dance months ago. The parched summer of wandering was a nightmare he longed to throw off, but it would cling to him till he was with his people.

At last he came to the great canyon that spread for miles like a gash worn by a huge serpent. He found his way down the north gorge trail, slipping and sliding in

the mud and rocks, and sighted the tipis scattered in the floor of the long deep canyon.

Cheyenne were there, some Comanche, and many Kiowa, probably all of that tribe that were not at Fort Sill with Kicking Bird, where Bright Mirror had gone.

Walker found Good Hands playing with a child, feeding it bits of pemmican. When she saw Walker, she looked past him and then back, as if she guessed what he had to tell her. She gave the child a farewell pat and came to meet her son.

"Where is your father, my son?"

Walker told her. She did not wail, though the scars she had made for First Son contracted, and a shine of hope died in her eyes. She must already have mourned for Spring Bull more sadly and bitterly than if he had died in battle.

She touched Walker as if to assure herself that he was real and led him into her lodge. Gone were the piles of fine robes and stuffed bags of food. She must have traded most of her belongings for food.

"Lie down, my son," she told him.

She brought him rabbit meat, a handful of dried plums, and a gourd of clear water and went to care for his horses; two of them he had now. When she came back, she carried his buffalo robe and spread it over heaped grass to make a second bed in the lodge while she told him the news.

First Son's mother had gone to live with a married sister and had become a wife of the brother-in-law. It was thought a good idea to marry sisters, since they were used to each other and not so likely to quarrel, but Spring Bull had married women from different families. Good

Chapter Four

Hands' brother had helped her, but it had been a very hard summer, and food was scarce for everyone.

Walker felt sorry for what his mother had endured, though he did not see what he could have done except follow his father through the season. He touched her bent shoulder.

"Do not worry, mother. I will hunt for you now."

Then he stretched out and slept soundly for the first time in months.

Good Hands did not wail or cut herself or even weep aloud, but next morning Walker noticed dried blood on her mouth, and when she spoke to him, he saw that she had knocked out two of her lower teeth.

Gray Owl came to the lodge. He smoked awhile in silence before he looked at Walker and spoke.

"My heart is glad to see you. But you are alone."

Walker told of the attack of the hunters and Spring Bull's cairn raised there on the Staked Plains. Gray Owl listened and smoked.

"Your father was a great chief," he said at last. "But he could not live without his son. I am happy that you have come back."

"Will the people stay in this canyon all winter?" Walker asked.

Gray Owl frowned. "Kiowa medicine men say their powers tell them the canyon is a good hideout from the white soldiers. You can see the tipis are up, and many of the women are getting new cedar lodge poles." The old chief's voice dropped. "I do not think we shall pass the winter in peace. I expect big trouble. What does your medicine tell you?"

Walker blinked. "Medicine? I have no medicine!"

Gray Owl peered at him closely, shrugged, then sighed. "It must be a different sort of medicine, one that does not speak to you."

"I do not have power," insisted Walker. "My father thought I would get some, but he said it would be—different, a strange kind."

"That must be it," agreed Gray Owl. "It must be power for the troubles that are blighting the Indians, a power you got while following your brother's bones and helping your father. Sometimes I fear the Great Spirit has forgotten his Indian children, but surely he has not—surely he will send us new power and new leaders." Gray Owl rose, looked deep into Walker's eyes. "You will be one of those men, Walker."

Even as a thrill tingled through him, Walker's heart weighed heavy. "Must we go to reservations?" he pleaded. "Must we live like the Caddo and Wichita, tame, beaten people?"

"Changes come. Once we had no horses. Once we had no guns or metal arrowheads. For a while we rode as lords of all the plains, living from buffalo, raiding and wandering as we pleased. Those times are gone, Walker."

"But—"

"Listen! The buffalo are dying. Even if there were no white men, we could not go on living off the herds, and there is not enough game of other kinds to feed all the Indians. Even if white men left us alone, soon we would either starve or settle in one main place to grow squash and corn and beans."

One of the most respected and powerful medicine men and chiefs talking like this? Walker could not believe

his ears. “If the whites who are killing the herds for their hides were gone, the buffalo would increase!” he protested. “All would be as before!”

Gray Owl bent to leave the lodge. “There is no end to white men, Walker. There are many across the great river and even more across a greater river. But there is an end to buffalo, and there may be an end to us.”

Walker, restless and almost angry at such gloom, got his bow and went up the canyon to hunt.

The old medicine man was depressed and worried, that was all. The spread of white men might be like a long, long severe winter, causing hardship, suffering, and some death, but it would not last forever. The white men would pass like a plague of grasshoppers, and the land would return to the Indians, to whom it had always belonged. Even before there were horses, even before there were guns!

Yet Walker hunted all that day and got nothing, not even a field mouse.

Walker roused to daybreak and the sound of firing. He thought drowsily that someone was out early for deer and settled deeper into his robe, but more shots followed and a far-off clamor of wails and shouting.

Tumbling out of bed, Walker seized his bow and arrows, thrust on his moccasins, and hurried out.

Men, women, children scurried past, only a few mounted. Horses, haltered to trees, plunged and whinnied. Pack animals ran about, half-fastened packs dragging under their bellies. Pursuing this confused mass pressed troopers, hundreds of them, with their pale faces and blue coats.

Only a few warriors clambered from the fleeing confusion to hide among the rocks and cedars on the canyon sides and shoot into the troopers. Walker doubled behind the lodge and ran stooped low till he came to a cluster of rocks. Dropping behind them, he shot down at the bluecoats, but it was too far, he was wasting arrows. He got up and ran through the scattered lodges, keeping to cover, hoping to find some rallied group of warriors.

How could so many whites have stolen up, making the dangerous descent down the canyon? There must have been no camp guards, and the sleep of the Indians had been sound, so sound there must have been no alarm, no time to paint for battle or organize. Walker watched, horrified, unbelieving, while warriors who had fought bravely all their lives fled with the women.

On the northwest side of the canyon women with babies and children were trying to climb the bluffs, some pulling up a few belongings with ropes. As the first panic subsided, most of the warriors checked their flight and began fighting. Those who could paint did so quickly and joined the battle.

Walker took heart, crouched in the best position handy, and sent his arrows down, then paused as vast herds of horses and mules charged down the canyon. Troopers were driving them! Walker saw his pony, First Son's war-horse, other familiar animals. Troopers in front pulled aside to let the herds through, and as they carelessly sat their mounts, some chief shouted, and all the warriors hidden along the canyon shot down.

A bugler fell. Troopers gathered him up and rode off, and they all retreated from the withering fire to shelter. The bluecoats could not ride up the canyon walls after

Chapter Four

the defenders, but neither were they eager to come on foot and leave their horses exposed.

So far as Walker could tell, no one was getting hit, either among troopers or Indians. They were just keeping each other pinned down, though down among the lodges soldiers were going through the tipis, collecting blankets, saddles, food, robes, and the lodges themselves.

All these things were placed in heaps and set aflame. Walker moaned with rage and dismay.

All the horses and mules had been driven off! Now shelter, food, and clothing were gone, too, and it was almost winter! There was no time to lay up even meager supplies for the dead season stretching ahead, and winter was in the best times a bleak period for Indians.

Nothing could be done. All the possessions of the Indians, Cheyenne, Kiowa, and Comanche, who had thought themselves safely hidden in this canyon, went up in fire and smoke.

Had Good Hands got safely up the canyon wall? Walker had not seen her. He grew hungrier, and thirst burned deep down his parched throat. He had shot away all his arrows.

The day wore on. About midafternoon the bluecoats retreated to the top of the canyon, and warriors began slowly assembling, dazed, unable to believe what had happened.

One Kiowa was dead, and the warriors took him up the bluff on one of the few remaining horses. Walker went to hunt for his own mother, with the wails of the Kiowa warrior's mother in his ears.

Good Hands was holding someone's young baby, feeding it broth from a cooking pot. She had somehow got a pack of belongings on their old mule no one would trade for, so from being among the poorest of the band, she was one of the few with a little food and clothing. Her scarred face lit up at sight of Walker, and he thought he would recognize her in the spirit world, holding a child or caring for someone.

She gave Walker a cup of broth and a bit of jerked meat. Twilight was falling. The wail of the Kiowa mother was heard through the huddled, miserable camp.

It was raining, slow, chilling, dismal. No one had a tipi. Good Hands gave away most of her food to people who had none at all.

Those who had saved a pack or robe slept on it, but many had to lie in puddles with cold rain slicing down like honed knives.

"Let's go see what the troopers have done with our herds," said Stands Tall, one of the bravest young chiefs. He had been a friend of First Son.

Walker joined the dozen young men who crept up on the bluecoat camp. The Indians' herds were enclosed by guards. No way of getting at them. Most of the young men went back to snatch what poor rest they could, but Walker stayed with Stands Tall to see if they might spot some way to steal back a few horses.

Comanche without horses were not Comanche!

When one of the bluecoats gave an order, Walker saw, without comprehension, how the soldiers raised their guns. He only understood when the troopers fired, loaded, and fired again into the massed animals.

The firing continued till all the horses, all the mules were dead, among them Walker's dun, companion of years and that terrible summer, and First Son's warhorse,

Chapter Four

who had not been sacrificed to accompany his young master but died now, without purpose, under the troopers' guns.

Such hatred welled in Walker that he would have burst from hiding, attacking the soldiers, had Stands Tall not caught his arm.

"We have only our lives left with which to fight," whispered the young chief. "Do not throw yours away!"

Slowly, in the downpour, they made their way back to their people.

Even after such a night, morning brought hope. Stands Tall said he intended to try to steal a few bluecoat horses. He did not choose to walk! Several other young men agreed, among them Gray Owl's nephew, Red Necklace. Walker looked at Good Hands.

"Do as you like," she urged him.

Gray Owl came up. "I will help your mother all I can," he told Walker. "We may have to go in to the reservation, but if you younger men can remount and stay on the plains, there may be hope for us to join you after the winter."

The leaders thought it best to break into groups in case the troopers harried them. Cheyenne went off one way, while the Kiowa took the opposite direction, and the Comanche drifted as seemed best. Walker, Stands Tall, and three other young men followed the troopers, and when the soldiers camped at night, the Indians crept toward where the horses were staked out.

They came with the wind against them to keep their scent from alerting the animals, but as each Indian selected his prize, the bay which Walker was approaching lifted its head and whinnied.

Walker undid its hobble and sprang on, stretched along its back. The horse bolted. Other horses, with Indians, shot past. There were shouts from the troopers and firing.

A fierce jolt. The horse stumbled. It must have run a hoof into a gopher hole. Walker fell off as the horse staggered and ran on.

Something smashed his leg, grazed his head. Walker tried frantically to crawl out of the way of oncoming hoofs, shouting troopers. He caught a clump of greasewood, dragged himself behind it, and the night went even blacker.

Chapter Five

Light pierced Walker's eyelids. He woke, not knowing where he was or remembering the night, but as he stirred, the dull ache in his leg pronged to red-hot pain, and he sucked in his breath sharply. His head throbbed, and he felt bruised and hurt all over.

All this took only a second, but he had moved in that instant of waking, and a cry rang out. White soldiers came running from their morning cook fire. One redheaded trooper swung a clubbed rifle. Close behind him was a stocky bald man.

Little honor in dying this way, but at least Walker had his knife. He drew it with his concealed hand and waited. *Good-bye, earth. Good-bye, sun. . . .*

He thrust himself upward, ignoring his smashed leg, as the redheaded soldier came close and caught at the trooper as the rifle struck his shoulder, knocking him sideways, jarring the knife from his grip.

Walker lay helpless, twisted to one side as the rifle butt crashed down, grazing his cheek. The dodge had been a desperate reflex; there was no hope. But a second, killing blow never came. Instead Walker heard a tone of command.

Looking up, he saw the bald man had caught the trooper's arm. The trooper argued, made a throat-slitting gesture, but the older man shook his head and spoke again in a commanding voice. The redhead shrugged. Glancing down at Walker, he muttered in Comanche, "This chief is a medicine man. He will help you—you Indian pup!"

Comanche from a red-haired, blue-eyed trooper? Walker gaped. "You—you speak my people's language!"

"I should! Lived in one of your stinking villages for five years after you durn Indians killed my folks!" The trooper shoved back his longish hair. The ear was gone. "See? My master trimmed that off the first time I ran away. He said next time it would be my liver, so I made sure not to get caught that time!" Another bluecoat had come up, rapping out questions, to which the redhead replied respectfully before turning to Walker. "Where are your people?"

Pain ran through Walker's leg like skewering irons, thrust into his brain. "Where are the leaves?" he asked the trooper. "Where is the summer?" He hoped Stands Tall and the others had got away, hoped they had stolen a few bluecoat horses, whatever happened now to him.

The bald medicine man gave orders. Walker was carried to a tent and placed on blankets. The bald chief felt all over the injured leg, took metal instruments and seemed to pick out bits of bone and dirt. Then he poured a stinging liquid over it. Walker ground his teeth.

A new kind of torture! But he would not flinch.

Chapter Five

Then the bald-head took a board and fastened the leg to it with strips of cloth. He offered Walker a tin cup of what Walker recognized as coffee, for he had now and then tasted it as a special treat obtained from white traders. Bald Head next gave him a piece of delicious fat fried meat and two strange hard little cakes, brown on the outside and white within.

While Walker munched these, the food warming him, giving strength and some bit of comfort, troopers came to carry him out to a wagon. Blankets had been spread among supplies, and as the men heaved and tugged to get him on the bed, Walker fainted.

He woke to the rattle and bump of the wagon. His leg jolted to fresh agony with every shift. Useless to think of escape till he could walk again or at least crawl. Fear gripped Walker, and he tried to raise himself, look at the shattered leg, but he could tell nothing about it because of the bandages.

Supposing he were crippled, would never walk easily again? Among Comanche there was no place for anyone who could not take care of himself.

That was when Walker remembered, sinkingly, that he was among bluecoats, not Comanche, and though they had spared his life for the moment, there was no way of guessing what torment or slavery they had in store.

After what seemed days, they stopped, and Walker smelled food. The redhead brought him a tin plate of beans and fat meat, a cup of strong black coffee.

"So you're still alive!" said the trooper in tones of regret.

"Where are we going?" Walker asked.

"Fort Sill. Now finish that food!"

So he was going to the fort. Maybe the soldiers would hang him there. Maybe they would let him join the reservation Indians. It might even be that Good Hands, Gray Owl, and the others would come in soon in order to eat through the winter now that their supplies were destroyed.

Walker burned in helpless anger at remembering the stacks of burning food, tipis, saddles, robes. But even worse was seeing again the way the horses had leaped and toppled, staggered and crumbled as the troopers shot them down.

By night, Walker burned with fever which carried him back to Adobe Walls or put him once again in the wake of a grief-stricken old man leading a war-horse which bore a skeleton wrapped in a yellow blanket. Again he shot an arrow into the streamers of the Sun Dance lodge, again he ran a hand across First Son's medicine bundle's contents to find no power there, again he saw the prophet Isatai astride his magic painted pony, and again he heard Spring Bull chanting at Medicine Bluff in a futile struggle to bring life back to his favorite son. Again Walker raised a cairn for his father and placed a yellow blanket in the dead arms.

He roused now and then to the trickle of water down his throat or the reviving heat of broth being spooned into his mouth while Bald Head propped him up. When he came out of the fever at last, exhausted and faint but clear-minded, he was in some kind of building lying on a narrow bed, with cloth draped all over him. Another bed was across from him. There was a table and a high, big wooden box in which were hung several bluecoat uni-

Chapter Five

forms and some shirts. Walker turned his head to stare wonderingly at the thick, bound masses of paper which white men could look at and get messages from, at a few framed pieces of decorated paper on the wall.

White man medicine. It must have much power.

The door opened. In came the red-haired trooper, followed by a nervous-looking Bright Mirror.

"You've got a visitor," grumbled the soldier to Walker. "And now you've got your mind back, I hope Doctor Miles sends you back where you belong, with the other heathen!" He propped himself on a chair and began to whittle a piece of wood. "Chatter away, you young varmints, but just remember I know what you're saying!"

Bright Mirror's eyes were full of pleasure and something near admiration. "So you live, friend! It is a long time since I left you at your camp after Adobe Walls."

"A long time," Walker agreed. "Do you know anything of the people who were camped in the great canyon?"

"They are coming in. All Cheyenne, Kiowa, and Comanche will have to, for the soldiers are driving them toward Fort Sill, not letting them rest, burning their lodges and killing their horses. Our people must either die or come to the reservation."

"Are no chiefs free?"

"Quanah Parker and his Quohada are still loose, but even for them there can be little time."

Walker turned his face to the wall till he could control his expression and not break down before the red-haired trooper. Could it really be true? Could the free life he had always known be over, not just for him but for all the plains people? If it were so, First Son was lucky.

New Medicine

"How is your leg?" Bright Mirror asked. "Can you walk?"

The trooper stirred. "Doctor Miles says he has to keep still till that bone knits, if it can."

"Doctor Miles is a good white man," Bright Mirror told Walker. "He tries to keep Indians alive, not kill us."

"Yes, sometimes I wonder whose side he's on," growled the redhead. He scratched his head where the ear was gone. "Fact is, Doc Miles don't care what color a sick person is. He's—well, you little heathens wouldn't understand, but he's a real good man even if he is an officer!"

A deep, pleasant voice boomed out just then, and Tim flushed, jumping up to salute, as the bald-headed man came in. He grew a gray tuft of hair between his nose and mouth, and his dark eyes held a twinkle as if he were truly pleased to see Walker was better. He spoke in a friendly tone, turning back the white cloths from Walker, and went over the leg with deft careful fingers. Nodding, he said something to the trooper, who looked a bit disappointed as he translated for Walker.

"Doctor Miles thinks you can try walking in a few days."

"Ask the doctor if my friend can stay with me," begged Bright Mirror.

The trooper shrugged, put a question to the doctor, who smiled broadly and said the Comanche word for yes. "Doc thinks if he's going to treat you heathen he should learn a bit of your language," the soldier explained disgustedly. "If the Comanche had treated him like they did me, he wouldn't care about their feelings? And the trooper began a glare at the boys which switched into a

Chapter Five

shamefaced grin. "Still and all, you're a tough little rascal," he said to Walker. "I'm glad you'll have the use of your leg!"

The first time Walker put weight on his leg, he almost toppled, but with Bright Mirror's help and a stick the redheaded trooper carved for him, he was soon able to get around fairly well, and Doctor Miles let him go home with Bright Mirror on a mule the Kiowa boy fetched.

The village of Kicking Bird, the great chief who was trying to get his people to live peaceably with the whites, was spread about much as it would have been off the reservation. The difference was that instead of hunting buffalo for food and roaming as they willed, these Indians drew rations and beef from the whites in return for agreeing to stay on the reservation and make no raids.

Bright Mirror's mother welcomed the boys and gave them bread made with white man's flour. Walker was hungry, yet it seemed to stick in his throat.

As his strength came back, he and Bright Mirror often went hunting. Bright Mirror's mother was a widow, who was always pleased at extra meat. One day the boys had shot two rabbits and were starting home when they noticed dust rising to the south. Gradually they saw moving figures—a few mules, a few horses, and straggling along on foot a horde of women, men and children, surrounded by bluecoats who drove them as buffalo might be pushed toward a cliff, to run over it and die.

Walker stared, frozen with grief and anger. He was too far away to tell if these were his band, but this was how they would eventually be forced in: driven like animals.

"What will happen to them at the fort?" he asked Bright Mirror.

"If the men have been fierce and are likely to cause trouble, they will be put in the icehouse or guardhouse. The families will stay on the flats of Cache Creek east of the post."

Walker turned his pony's head. "I must go see if my mother is there."

"If you join them, the soldiers will keep you there. Stay with me, friend! Our food is better, and we are not crowded. Later you can visit your mother."

"If she is there, I must see her now."

"Well, I will ride with you as close as we can so you will not tire your leg. I'm afraid to let you keep the horse, since the soldiers might take it away."

The boys rode within hailing range. "Thank you, friend," Walker told Bright Mirror. He climbed down and gave the reins to his companion. Bright Mirror handed him both rabbits.

"Here, these will make someone a meal. I will visit the new camp as soon as it is permitted."

The young Kiowa rode off. Walker limped forward. Troopers looked at him but let him by. They had already herded the warriors off to the prisons and were bringing the women and children into a big stone corral.

Most of the people looked too tired and trapped to lament, but here and there a woman wailed or a child cried out in loneliness or fear. Walker spoke to a few he recognized, trying to cheer them, telling them they would soon be let out of the corral to make a new camp.

At last he found Good Hands. She sat huddled in a blanket, rocking a girl child of about three who fretted and

Chapter Five

sobbed. When she saw him, Good Hands stiffened, then put down the child, and ran to him, weary eyes glowing.

"My son! You are not dead!"

"No, I was wounded, but a white medicine man healed my leg, and I have been with Bright Mirror, my Kiowa friend."

"And you have brought meat! Oh, it is good to have a hunter again!"

Good Hands took the rabbits and skinned them quickly, while Walker made a fire. All the time the little girl tossed and cried like a sick bird. "Who is that?" Walker asked. He did not like to play with children, but his mother was busy, and he wanted to hush the girl, so he held her and tried rocking her to and fro as Good Hands had done.

"She is a Cheyenne child. Her mother died on the way from the great canyon and I could not bear to leave the little thing to cry herself to death in the bushes."

Babies, like old people, might be thrown away in hard times, when there was not enough food and they became a heavy burden. Walker knew that the sensible thing for Good Hands to have done was mind her own business, but he was somehow glad she had not. She would probably have saved even a white child if she found one in trouble!

The girl had quieted, but her little face felt burning hot. "Is she sick?" Walker asked.

"A bad fever," said Good Hands. She stirred the rabbit stewing in the iron pot she had carried all the way from the canyon. "I have had nothing nice to feed her. Broth should help."

It seemed to. Good Hands shared the stew with

those who had nothing, and soon they all lay down to sleep as best they could.

The little girl whimpered through the night in spite of all that Good Hands could do, and by morning the child breathed with a shuddering terrible sound, broken with coughing, that sounded as if she could not live.

"The white medicine man who helped you," Good Hands said at last. "Could he help Meadowlark?" That was the name she had given the tiny girl.

"I will see," decided Walker.

He took the girl and went to the gate of the yellow-white stone corral. A trooper stopped him there.

"Doctor Miles," Walker said. It was all the English he knew. He pointed to the baby. "Doctor Miles!"

The trooper roared something and started to shove Walker back, but a man shouted, and in a minute the redheaded soldier came up. He spoke to the guard and squinted curiously at Walker.

"What are you doing here, spalpeen?"

"My mother is here," Walker said. "She is taking care of this girl, who is very sick. I thought the white medicine man might help her."

"Doc can't fret about every papoose that gets a cough," the trooper said. The girl went into a spasm of tight, wracking coughs, and the redheaded man looked at her with reluctant pity. He spoke to the guard and nodded to Walker. "Come along, heathen. We'll see what Doc can do."

They found the doctor in his quarters. He examined the child and spoke grimly to the trooper, who told Walker, "She has a bad chest sickness. The doctor will see if one of the officers' wives will nurse her."

Chapter Five

"But my mother—"

"Your mother does not have a warm house or a way to do what is necessary to save the child. You'd better hope," went on the trooper sharply, "that some white lady will take the trouble, or this girl will be dead before morning!"

"How will we know how she is?" Walker persisted.

The trooper spoke to the doctor, who was wrapping Meadowlark in a blanket. The doctor put an arm on Walker's shoulder, said a few words.

"Doc says you can come here every day about sundown and he'll tell you how the girl is. He'll get word to the guards to let you out of the corral."

Walker looked at Meadowlark's fever-bright eyes. Such a tiny thing to hold so much sickness!

"Tell the doctor we are grateful," Walker said and followed the doctor outside.

"You don't really have to go back to the corral," said the trooper grudgingly. "That's only for the wild Indians, till we get 'em sorted out and tamed down a bit."

"That is where my mother is," said Walker and started for the big rock pen.

Chapter Six

It was a good thing they did not have sick little Meadowlark to nourish and keep warm during the next days, for there was scarcely room to build a cook fire and no way to keep really sheltered.

A kind of roof jutted out from the sides of the corral, running all the way around the enclosure, leaving a bare gap in the center. This had been built to protect foaling mares and their colts from the weather. It was not much help to families already exhausted from a long flight across the plains, families whose possessions were nearly all destroyed.

Every day soldiers counted the people to make sure none had escaped. Then a few beefs were turned in. These were slaughtered in the middle of the corral, cut up, and divided among the prisoners. Good Hands still had her cooking pot and made broth with her and Walker's shares, but most of the people had to eat their rations uncooked, and it was tough, stringy meat to start with. Good Hands carried broth to those who were too sick or weak to eat the beef. She gave her strength to whoever needed it.

As Walker followed her with the cooking pot and did whatever he could to ease or cheer the ailing, he began to think that Good Hands, a squaw—and not even Spring Bull's favorite—was braver than many a great chief.

She did not paint for battle, or count coups, or own power of the kind granted by spirits and governed by tabus, but she had some kind of medicine in her fingers, quick to find and rub away an ache, and a kind of power in her quiet sympathy and gentle voice.

Such thoughts were crazy. They should not be in the mind of a warrior, and Walker tried to scoff them away, but they grew stronger, especially when he had to see that the best warriors were locked up and those left in the corral were good for nothing now but to kill the cattle.

Each evening Walker went to the doctor's quarters, where the redhead would translate news of Meadowlark. A white chief's wife had taken her and was caring tenderly for the child under the doctor's instructions. By the end of the week, Walker was able to assure Good Hands that the little girl would live.

A few days later, after some commotion at the gate, Doctor Miles came in with a white woman. The redheaded trooper, Corporal Timothy Duveen, strode to one side, clearing a way.

"Walker!" he shouted, for he had finally learned Walker's right name instead of calling him always heathen or spalpeen. "Walker, fetch your mother! Doctor Miles has brought Major Harris' lady to talk to her."

Walker found Good Hands rubbing Stands Tall's mother's back. This old woman always complained of an

Chapter Six

ache there, and not even the best medicine man had been able to cure her.

"I have already cut her back and sucked out five stones," said Gray Owl. "A squaw's rubbing won't help her if that did not!"

Stands Tall's mother just groaned.

"Maybe your medicine won't work here," Stands Tall said gloomily to Gray Owl.

"The doctor who cured my leg is here," Walker said. "Shall I ask if he will see your mother, Stands Tall?"

The woman really howled at that. "He would kill me!" she wailed. "He would put some bad white spirit in me!"

"How can he cause you more pain than you have now?" demanded Stands Tall. "Yes, Walker, bring him if he will come. At least he may give us something good to eat and more blankets."

So Walker escorted Good Hands to where the white people waited. Corporal Duveen explained that Mrs. Major Harris wanted to keep Meadowlark, bring her up like a white girl. Would Good Hands consent? And would Good Hands like to visit the child today and see that she was indeed getting strong and well?

"I will visit Meadowlark first," decided Good Hands, shrewdly studying the white woman's face.

Mrs. Harris had hair that was so blond it was almost white, though she looked very young. Her gray eyes were kind, and she had a smiling kind of mouth, though she was looking about the corral with tight-set lips and an expression of shock.

She said something to Doctor Miles which Duveen did not translate, but his one ear got red, and he stood straighter and stiffer than ever.

New Medicine

"Please ask the doctor if he will look at a sick woman," Walker said. "She moans a lot, and no one can help her."

The doctor and Duveen came with Walker after seeing Mrs. Harris and Good Hands out of the corral. Stands Tall glared at the corporal. Gray Owl, arms folded, was waiting to judge how good the white medicine man was.

"Gray Owl is our best medicine man," Walker told Duveen. "He says this woman has little stones in her gall bladder, just like a deer or buffalo gets in its gall bladder, and that these stones hurt her. He has cut in her back and sucked some out, but she still is in pain."

As Duveen translated, Doctor Miles nodded and raised his eyebrows respectfully toward Gray Owl. "Please tell the medicine man that I will need his help. Maybe together we can cure the woman."

Gray Owl did not answer. In fact he looked reproachfully at Walker as if blaming him for describing the woman's illness. Doctor Miles knelt and pressed here and there on the woman. She was too frightened to speak, but several times she gave a gasp of pain. Miles rose, frowning.

"He thinks it is gall stones, just like the medicine man says," announced Duveen. "But he has a different way of cutting and getting at the stones and thinks that might make her well. He cannot cut here, though. She must come to the hospital."

"People die in that big house," objected Stands Tall.

"And the place is not purified or cleansed of the bad power afterwards," added Gray Owl.

"I won't go there!" howled the woman, sitting up and grasping her son's knees. "Oh, my son, don't let them

take me to the white people's place to die! I would rather die here!"

"But you don't have to die," said Walker. "I got well. I hardly have a limp! And Meadowlark, the little Cheyenne girl, is getting over that terrible coughing." He looked apologetically at Gray Owl. "It must be that Gray Owl's medicine doesn't like it here and won't work."

Gray Owl nodded. "That is it. I must get some new medicine. But your mother cannot wait on that, Stands Tall. She must go to the white place-to-be-sick-in."

She howled, but Stands Tall helped her to her feet and said sternly, "You must go. I will come with you if the soldiers permit." Duveen queried the doctor, who hesitated a moment and then shrugged, making a gesture that included Gray Owl.

"Doctor Miles says both Stands Tall and the medicine man can come. If they see things are all right at the hospital, it should be easier to get other sick Indians to stay there." Duveen studied Walker. "You might as well tag along. I'll take you to Major Harris' and do any translating that's needed between Mrs. Major Harris and your mother. Fine chance for that papoose, it is!"

So with Stands Tall supporting his mother, the little procession moved through the staring Indians to the gate. Stands Tall's mother gave a stifled wail now and then, but her son admonished her, and she did seem to draw comfort from his presence and that of Gray Owl. If the white medicine man meant evil to her, he would hardly have invited her son and the best medicine man of her tribe.

At the hospital, Duveen and Walker left Doctor Miles with his patient, Stands Tall, and Gray Owl. Duveen shoved back his red hair from the earless side.

"Doc's a better Christian than soldier," he grumbled. "That old squaw won't appreciate it if he saves her, and if she dies anyway, that son of hers may stick an ax in him, while that befeathered old heathen will make some wild tale about how dangerous white medicine men are. No hard feelings, Walker me lad—I've got fond of you in a sneaking kind of way—but the only sensible way to deal with you heathen is to wipe you out. You won't be happy on reservations, no more'n any wild things are in pens."

"So you'd kill us like deer or buffalo?"

"It's kinder in the long run than fencing you in."

"And quicker."

Duveen grinned. "Well, spalpeen! You've spunk. You may do. A lot of you young ones may. But how about the warriors, young bucks trained for war and the hunt and nothing else? Everything they believed worthwhile is gone, or will be in a year or two."

"Maybe—" Walker's bottled hopes burst out. He would not have voiced them to another Indian, but he could say them to this white trooper. "Maybe a real prophet will come to us—one who will know how to shove the whites away and dance back the buffalo! Maybe all will be as it was—"

The trooper shook his head. "Laddie, east of these plains there's only whites, many, many more than all the Indians put together, and more come all the time from lands beyond a great water. There's no way to be rid of them. So they'll be rid of you one way or another."

Walker pondered this. "There must be a way for Indians to live. There must be some power, some medicine, left for us!"

Chapter Six

"Maybe." Duveen gave a hard bright smile. "But it won't be by slicing off white men's ears and taking their scalps." They turned down a walk, and the trooper knocked on a door, his face softening as Mrs. Harris came to the door and asked them inside.

Meadowlark nestled against the white woman's shoulder, her big dark eyes clear of fever now, her long hair clean and brushed, hanging down a pretty pink dress. She smiled shyly when Walker spoke to her, hiding her face on Mrs. Harris' arm. Walker thought with a pang that it was as if he were the stranger to the Indian child, not the white woman.

And is this what will happen? Will they take our children and make them like whites?

Such thoughts buzzed in Walker's head like angry bees. It was a relief to see Good Hands. She sat on a rug by a fireplace, drinking and eating. The things smelled good. Walker's stomach contracted, and his mouth watered.

Mrs. Harris asked something with a smile. "She says would you like something to eat," Duveen said disapprovingly.

Walker sat down by Good Hands and waited, while Meadowlark curled up in a big bench with a back and arms and cushions. Mrs. Harris brought a plate and a cup of steaming coffee. There was bread, crusty and spread with a delicious yellow grease, and several things that looked like bird eggs, only much bigger.

"Those are from a squaw hen," Good Hands told him. "Mrs. Major Harris is giving me a squaw hen and some eggs for her to hatch so that we can have eggs like this every day. Until my chickens lay, she will give us

eggs for the sick, the babies, and the old. And she has squaw cows, too. She will give us milk."

"Milk is only for babies!" Walker objected.

"It is very good for children and the old," Good Hands told him severely. "Now that we cannot live off buffalo, we must find new ways of keeping strong. You are eating the squaw hen's eggs fast enough!"

Walker finished his plate and changed the subject. "Meadowlark looks like a white child."

"It is a pretty dress."

"But it is a white girl's dress."

"Can you find her antelope skin to make a nice tunic?"

Duveen cackled. "She's too sharp for you, laddie! Come along and I'll show you where the cows are."

"Unless they are for beef, I don't care where they are!"

Good Hands looked at Walker as if she could not believe her ears. "My son, have you not heard children crying because they are hungry and the beef is too strong? Have you not heard the toothless old ones sucking a hunk of stringy meat for whatever nourishment they can get?"

Shamed as much by what she said as by being addressed so by a woman, Walker shuffled and moved for the door. Before he could reach it, Mrs. Harris brought him a large jug. She spoke to him, smiling, pushing a stray lock of that peculiar hair back into place. It really was silver! Yet she looked so young. Maybe she had some kind of medicine that kept wrinkles from coming.

"Come along," said Duveen to Walker, bowing deep first to Mrs. Harris, though he did not seem the kind of man to be much impressed by any squaw.

Chapter Six

Once outside, the trooper peered into Walker's jug. "Sure, it's milk! You're to give it to those who need it most. Then if you'll come to the shed tonight, I'll fill the jug again—and teach you to milk so you can get your own each night and morning."

"*You* milk?"

"It's not my job, but you just bet I can do it! It was one of my chores back home, before you heathen killed my family and made a slave of me." Duveen scowled. "Funny. Mrs. Harris, now, she's a right to hate you Indians, as good a right as me. Yet she's adopting that little gal! Sending milk to the corral, giving hens—I wonder the Major doesn't put his foot down!"

"What does she have against Indians?" Walker asked.

"You've noticed that white, white hair?"

Walker nodded.

"Well, when Mrs. Harris was sixteen, she was goldenhaired as a sunset I'm told, bonny and gay, one of three daughters to a colonel. They were traveling with their mother to join the colonel at a new post when Comanche attacked the coach—killed the escort, scalped the mother and two younger girls, carried off Mrs. Harris. It was two weeks before her father could track down the band that had stolen her. She had gone dumb—couldn't speak, seemed to have lost her mind. When she finally did start remembering and knowing where she was, it's said she screamed for hours on end. And she had gone completely white in those two weeks. Major Harris was one of the officers who helped rescue her—young lieutenant he was then." Duveen rubbed his missing ear. "Reckon maybe that's why he's patient with her notions, humors her a bit."

He pointed at some sheds with cows grazing near. "Well, laddie! Will you meet me here tonight?"

Walker shifted the heavy jug on his arm. A warrior, milking cows? Then he thought of the old, the sick, the children—of Good Hands, Meadowlark, and Mrs. Harris with her white hair.

"I'll come," he said and wondered why Duveen's eyes grew fiercer and brighter before the red-haired man grinned and clapped him on the shoulder.

"Why, if I can teach you to milk a cow, maybe there's hope for you heathen yet! Now you better get that milk passed out before it goes sour!"

Chapter Seven

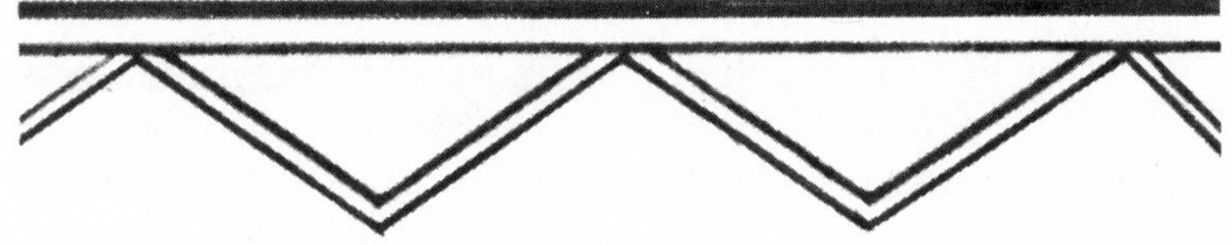

A few days later the Indians in the corral were counted and allowed to camp on the flats of Cache Creek to the east of the fort. As new bands of Kiowa and Comanche drifted in to give themselves over to the mercy of the Great White Father, their horses and mules were taken away, along with their weapons and camp gear. Much of their property was heaped up and burned. The horses and mules were driven out west of the post and shot by the hundreds till the stench carried by the evening breeze grew so bad that the bluecoat commander halted the slaughter and had the animals sold.

"The red-haired trooper says the money from the sales will someday go to the Indians who owned the horses," sneered Stands Tall, who was growing restless like many of the other warriors. He was much better off than the chiefs camping in pup tents within the walls of the unfinished icehouse east of the post. Walker had seen an Army wagon drive up to the guarded door and watched soldiers toss chunks of raw meat over the walls as if they were feeding dangerous wild beasts.

"Who will pay for the hundreds of horses given the Tonkawa scouts and white volunteers?" growled another warrior. "Those Tonkawa! They eat people! They are worse than the whites because they serve them!"

"I never saw so many horses and mules," Duveen exclaimed one evening when Walker joined him at the shed. "Must be seventy-five hundred head at least! Major Harris says they're worth a quarter million dollars, but they won't start to fetch that around here where the buyers are poor and the sale's forced."

"I don't know your numbers and money," said Walker. "But it sounds very much—too much to lose."

"You can only lose as much as you have," said Duveen. "My folks lost everything, even their scalps."

Walker glanced up from the cow he was trying to milk. It still seemed outlandish to him to get milk from these big-eyed, tail-switching creatures rather than lance them for a splendid feast. The cow had refused to let down her milk the first few times Walker sat by her, but she was getting used to him now, and he was becoming more practiced, so that with much labor he could coax several cups of milk before Duveen took over and finished with quick skilled jerking squeezes.

"Duveen, would you rather see your family living as my people are?"

"Lad, while there's life, there's hope for better days."

"There can be no better days for the Indians. Only changed ones, without the buffalo. All our years will be like one long starving winter."

"You're young. You can learn new ways."

Chapter Seven

Walker did not answer but worked for the milk he would take back to children who would have to grow up in that dying winter season of his people and to old people who would many of them not survive the snows that would soon fall.

Duveen finished filling the pail. He gave the cow a pat on the flank and turned her out in the pasture. That was what he must have done as a young boy on his parents' farm before he was captured and his ear cut off.

"Thank you, Duveen," Walker said suddenly. Surprise lit the trooper's face. Walker hurriedly took the bucket and went back to camp.

He took the milk around to those who most needed it and then went home to the shelter of canvas and willow Good Hands had made. She looked up from stirring broth made from their meat ration, a slow, delighted smile broadening her face.

"Look!" She went inside and from their one remaining storage bag produced a beautiful brown egg. "Our hen laid it today! Soon the eggs Mrs. Harris gave us will hatch into chickens, and they will lay, too!"

"That is very good," nodded Walker, viewing the hen who lived at the back of their lodge with more respect and enthusiasm than he had felt before. "When she has laid all her eggs, we can eat her."

"That will be a while," retorted Good Hands. "Can you milk the cow yet by yourself?"

"She still does not like my smell," said Walker. "And my hands are trained to a bow, not to milking. But I do a little better each day."

"What is this you do better?" demanded a familiar, laughing voice. Bright Mirror stood in the entrance.

New Medicine

"Come in, friend," said Good Hands.

He did, stopped short to stare at the hen, whose eyes glittered orange as she settled protectively on her nest and made a soft clucking murmur.

"Where did you get the chicken?" he asked.

"Mrs. Harris gave me the squaw hen," said Good Hands, proudly producing the wonderful egg. "See what we got today? Soon our squaw hen will hatch baby chicks, which will grow up to lay many eggs. There will be many to give away."

"Mrs. Harris?" Bright Mirror's brow furrowed. "Ah! She is the one who is turning the little Indian girl into a white child, dressing her in white clothes, teaching her white ways!"

"She is the one who nursed little Meadowlark and saved her life," rebuked Good Hands.

"I do not think it is good to save her life if she must stop being Indian," said Bright Mirror. "If Meadowlark were my sister, I would rather see her dead!"

"Then it is a good thing she is not your sister!" scolded Good Hands. "That is a bad thing to say, friend. You have no right to choose how another person should live. Now sit down and eat. I do not want any more of such talk!"

For a moment it seemed Bright Mirror would turn and go, but Good Hands put a cup of broth in his hands and gave each boy a piece of stringy beef. They ate in a silence that grew more comfortable.

"You have cooked it well," said Bright Mirror, with a return of his usual good manners. Then his face grew dark and his voice harshened. "It will never taste like buffalo, though. Our whole camp stinks of beef. It is in our systems till we almost moo like cattle—white men's cattle!"

Chapter Seven

"We must eat something," said Walker.

Bright Mirror jumped to his feet. "Somewhere there must still be herds!" he cried fiercely. "The white hunters cannot have killed them all!"

"Maybe they have," argued Walker, talking against what he hoped as well as against Bright Mirror. "Have you seen any buffalo this fall? Except for one old bull who was being torn apart by coyotes, I have not seen any buffalo since those we saw slaughtered on the way to Adobe Walls."

"Well, I am going on a hunt," insisted Bright Mirror. He smiled, and something in his look made Walker afraid for his friend. Living on the reservation had not been good for the once gay Kiowa. "Come with me, Walker!"

"There will be no buffalo."

"Then I may find a white man instead," flashed Bright Mirror. His white teeth showed, and the silver ornaments he still wore in his hair danced and gleamed in the twilight. "Several chiefs are still out, still raiding! Big Bow, Lone Wolf, Poor Buffalo of the Kiowa, and plenty of Comanche besides Quanah! Come with me, Walker. A little time of freedom is better than a long life under the white men."

Walker's blood danced. He went outside, stared past the miserable huddled camp toward the end of the mountains, with Texas south and the great Staked Plain westward, the open country of his people and the other horse Indians. How beautiful the land was, even in its winter bareness! The naked trees stood out against each other, green bark of willows against gray cottonwoods and the reddish brown of scrub oak, while tufts of green grass showed against the sere yellow, and gashes of red earth seemed to Walker like the bared arms of his mother soil.

To live out there—roam wild again?

He and Bright Mirror together could find enough food. They might elude the bluecoats all their lives, might even someday get back part of what had been stolen from their people, organize a new, hard-hitting band of desperate warriors who could shelter in the great mountains where the Ute lived or in some stronghold like that big canyon in Texas—

Where the horses and mules had been shot and the wealth of the villages burned, where warriors had fled, tripping over women and children?

But even if Walker and Bright Mirror could stay at large, how would that help their people? Walker almost groaned as he glanced away from the shining rim of the mountains to the tents and shelters scattered across the flats. He had taken milk and broth to nearly every family at one time or another in the past two weeks. He knew the misery and hopelessness of the old, the bewildered wretchedness of the children.

How could he go and forget them?

But it was so little! To carry some milk or a cup of broth, loan a blanket or fetch Good Hands to help in a particularly serious case.

Walker looked up at the sky. *I don't ask to be a warrior! he cried silently to whatever powers were there. I don't ask for medicine! I ask only to be able—somehow—to help my people!*

He stood like that, stretched between earth and heaven, to call some power down. Nothing answered. There were only the muffled sounds of captive people, the sickening stench from the west of over seven hundred slaughtered horses and mules.

Chapter Seven

Bright Mirror touched his shoulder. "Friend, brother! Come with me!"

"I cannot."

Bright Mirror drew back. "You—you are afraid!"

Walker bit back the retort that he had followed a dead warrior's bones when Bright Mirror had not wished to. "I am going to Medicine Bluff and pray for power," he said. "I need—I need a vision, friend, I need strength."

"You need buffalo meat," scoffed Bright Mirror. "You have been shut up too long with women and children! What you need is to get back among free warriors."

"I hope it goes well with you and that you find a herd," said Walker. "Spend the night. My mother has good broth and meat."

No Indian especially liked to be abroad at night by himself. Even if one was too old to believe in Big Cannibal Owl, with whom small children were frightened, it was only prudent to beware of restless spirits. Walker had bent to enter the shelter, when Bright Mirror's voice stopped him.

"I will go back to my camp. I do not want to stay here and catch whatever it is that makes your blood like water! And I shall think about Meadowlark. She does not belong with the whites!" He vaulted onto the back of his pony and galloped off. Soon he was only an echoing sound in the dusk.

Slowly Walker unclenched his hands. It hurt for Bright Mirror to think him a coward! It galled to stay in this smelly forlorn camp prison!

Tomorrow he would go to Medicine Bluff. If the spirits had any regard for the Indians, surely they would speak to him, give him some secret or way to help his people.

New Medicine

As soon as he had milked next morning and given the bucket's contents to those most in need, he took his pipe, tobacco, flint, and since they had not a single one of Good Hands' beautifully tanned buffalo robes left, he took an Army blanket instead. The spirits might not like that, but they had not protected the Indians' possessions, and could not, in fairness, blame Walker for seeking them while wrapped in a white man's blanket.

"I am going to ask for medicine," he told Good Hands. "Duveen says he will bring or send the milk while I am gone if you will see to giving it out."

"Oh, my son! I have tanned so many fine robes, and now there is not even a shabby old one for you!"

"The spirits must take me as I am," Walker said.

The Indians camping about the post were allowed considerable freedom so long as they looked peaceful, and Walker, stripped to breechcloth and moccasins, with the blanket draped against the chill wind, did not look dangerous. No soldiers tried to stop him.

Was it good to go back where Spring Bull had vainly tried to pray life back into his favorite son? Walker felt a coldness along his spine at the memory but made himself walk on. More warriors had got strong medicine at Medicine Bluff than at any other place, and all plains tribes knew of wonders connected with the spot.

Twice, on his way, he stopped to smoke. Even though he had no robe, he must try to follow the ritual as faithfully as he could. But he lacked any feeling that his prayers were heard, had no sense of an answering presence.

Was there power anymore for Indians? Had the spirits deceived Spring Bull in promising a new medicine to

Chapter Seven

Walker? Walker scarcely dared to hope for favor, yet he had to. Hope, beyond their bare lives, was all his people had; hope that somehow they could learn to live in the new ways.

Falling darkness played tricks with shadows as Walker wrapped himself in his blanket. Coldness touched his bones, and his scalp prickled. This was where many medicine men had got power. Scores of them were buried all around. Their ghosts might be roaming—or that of First Son, who had been brought here in Spring Bull's futile attempt to pray him back to life. But though the shadows darkened and danced, no real eerie shape glided toward Walker, and more earthly thoughts crowded into his mind.

Ten years ago the chiefs and soldiers had made a treaty which promised to the Indians forever the lands beyond the Mississippi and below the Kansas. What the whites never understood was that one chief might promise till his war paint streaked, but he could not bind his own band to honor his promise, much less speak for the whole tribe.

Who could speak for the Comanche, Cheyenne, or Kiowa? Even the greatest war chiefs held influence only so long as they were respected and believed in, but they held no actual power after a raid, and the peace chiefs always led by personality and prestige.

White soldiers had to obey a commander whether he was a fool or not. Indians would not. Each warrior could join a war party or stay home if he wished. It was up to him. A treaty signed by one chief did not bind even his band, much less a tribe. It all seemed perfectly plain and natural.

New Medicine

What Walker could not understand was why the white leaders, who did speak for Washington and the whites, never kept their part of the treaties. White people swarmed west into Indian lands, breaking one solemn agreement after another. Words could not hold them, and they had the numbers and the guns.

Was there any hope for the Indian? Any way to live free, even if it could not be in the old beloved fashion?

All that night Walker held himself ready for the spirits. Mostly he peered into the darkness, willing for something to come forth, but now and then he drowsed or stirred from cramping. It was cold. The blanket was far from being as warm and wind tight as a buffalo robe.

Each time Walker heard a rustle or saw a hint of movement, he held his breath, and his heart tripped fast. Would the power come at last, would his guardian spirit finally speak?

The rustling always faded; the shape vanished; the wings shot past, and still he waited.

At dawn, sick at heart and faint with hunger, he washed and prayed to the Four Directions. As he gazed westward, toward the plains beyond the mountains, he wondered where Bright Mirror was, if he was, in his quest, having better luck. It would be good anyhow, whatever happened later, to ride west like that, far from the soldiers and miserable camp on the flats!

In a wave of lonely disgust, Walker knew he did not want this new medicine even if it could be had.

He wanted the old medicine—the kind of power Indians had always used to help in raids and healing, the sort that had belonged to Spring Bull and made him a mighty chief.

Chapter Seven

If there was no more of that—if it was used up, or if it had been killed by the coming of the white men, then there was no medicine worth having!

Walker dropped his blanket and ran to where he could look far away, far into the lands where his people had roamed from the first remembered times.

Some Indians were still out there, roving like blue-eyed Quanah and his band. If Walker joined such a group or found Bright Mirror, he could stay out for years, possibly his whole life, refuging in some natural stronghold and living off settlers' cattle if the buffalo never came back. A few warriors would be able to elude the strongest force of soldiers, who could not permanently guard every ravine, every canyon which Indians knew so well.

But the families—women, old men, and children—they could not hide from the soldiers, live again off the reservation. And what would happen to them without husbands, sons, fathers?

Slowly, drooping, Walker went back to his vigil place. He smoked and prayed, fearful that his flare of rebellion had offended the strange new medicine so it would not visit him.

I am sorry, he told it. I cannot help my heart. I cannot help wanting to be free, longing to range outside the fence. But pity the others even if you are angry with me—pity them, and give me hope to take to them!

But the power did not come.

All that day Walker thought of Good Hands, Gray Owl, the children, their mothers, the sick and despairing, all those penned in the dreary camp by the fort. He held them strong in his mind before the powers, and at sunset he prayed again, smoking in the four directions. As he

wrapped in his blanket, he faced east, hoping that before sunrise he would meet the new medicine, carry it back as a sign of love from the Great Spirit for his red children, a promise that their misery would pass.

It was colder even than the night before, but though he was far from comfortable, Walker's head nodded with weariness. Each time his chin fell forward, he jerked erect, forcing his protesting eyelids open. He must not be asleep if the power came.

The first thing he saw was a pale glimmering in the east. Instead of the lift of heart he usually felt at the dawn, even in the prison camp, Walker was gripped with disappointment so bitter and complete that he clenched his hands and clamped his teeth hard together.

No sign. No power!

He had tried hard. There must just not be any power left for Indians. After all, First Son had not got a vision, either. Medicine, Indian medicine, must be dried up, finished.

He might as well go after Bright Mirror, live out his own life, at least, in freedom. He stood up, weak and stiff from his futile watch, and folded his blanket, already planning to make his way to the End of the Mountains and from there to the Staked Plain.

But what of the people? Those women back in camp with their children were the life of the tribe, the future of the Comanche. Walker hung his head in anguish and grief.

If there was no way for the Indians, was it not best that the tribe die out now rather than live on like diseased coyotes, ill with mange, whose teeth were gone?

Something deep within Walker rebelled at the

thought. The Great Spirit was good. He could not mean to send all his red children under. He must have help for them, a new way, some means by which they could live near white men.

Oh, New Medicine! Come to me! he prayed, stretching out his arms, straining for the gift, the promise.

Nothing came.

Lowering his arms, he stood weaving from fatigue, hunger, angry despair. The sun edged up through clouds, cracking the sky with fire. Then a rustling in the bush made Walker whirl.

Chapter Eight

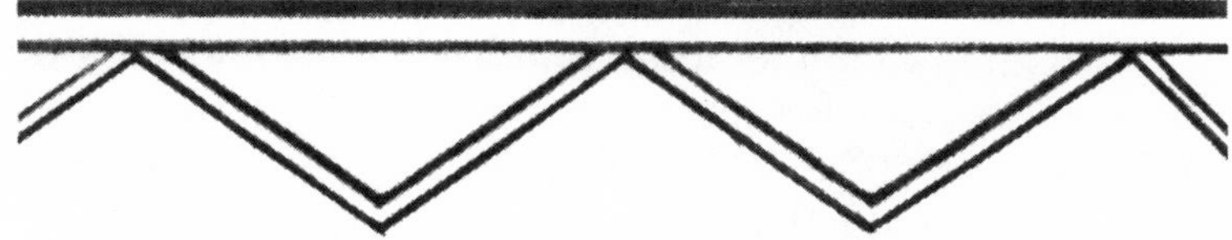

The power!

Walker's breath came in a rush, painfully, and then he didn't breathe at all as the willows shook and he heard the crackling of twigs and undergrowth. A glimpse of brown—not a bear, surely! That would be very strong power!

There was a thrusting of branches, and a muzzle came into view, followed by the gaunt body of a horse.

So this was the answer to Walker's long wait! A horse red of eye with ribs that stood out like tipi poles, a horse whose hair was worn off to the hide in many places, who could never have been handsome, what with his scrawny neck, pigeon toes, and muzzle hooked like the beak of an eagle! Walker fought a savage impulse to punish him for his disappointment, drive him back into the willows with blows and shouts.

The animal was very sick. He eyed Walker, head dragging low, and Walker saw the furrow running under his belly and an oozing wound in one shoulder.

New Medicine

"Hua, horse," said Walker softly, ashamed now of his first anger. "Let me look at you."

The horse eyed Walker distrustfully but let him come near. Examining the furrow, Walker found it almost healed. The ragged pus-edged wound in the shoulder was the trouble. Little splinters of bone seemed to be working their way out, and the bloody ooze smelled foul and drew flies and gnats which further added to the animal's discomfort by swarming at his eyes.

This must be one of the hundreds of horses shot by the soldiers. Left for dead, he had dragged himself into the brush and still clung to life, in spite of the shoulder.

Well, thought Walker to any power that might hear: *You did not send medicine, but a creature needing medicine! You sent no answer but more trouble! So I must see what I can do without your help!*

He found some broad mullein leaves and cleaned the wound with them, speaking gently to the animal as he worked. The horse stood patiently, as if he somehow understood that Walker wanted to help. Plainly, his Indian owner had misused him, for his hide was welted with old scars, but there was a strength, a toughness in the horse that commanded Walker's admiration.

"Maybe I can help you," Walker told him, patting his tangled mane. "You must get well—show those bluecoat soldiers that you outlived their bullets!"

He led the horse to drink in the creek, then gathered handfuls of the sparse grass and brought it to the animal so that he could feed without much moving around. Walker crushed mullein leaves into a pulp and stuffed this into the wound to help draw out the poison.

"I will come see you every day and help you get grass, horse. It was a good thing for you I came on a med-

Chapter Eight

icine quest!" He gave the animal a farewell caress, collected his blanket and pipe, and started to the camp.

Need to help the survivor had called up all Walker's reserve energy, and as the lift of heart he had felt in aiding it subsided, weariness and hunger possessed him.

Two days and nights wasted! Worst of all, he had no further glimmer of hope for medicine, a strong gift of power from the spirits. As he neared the camp, Walker's mood grew heavier with each dragging step.

Were his people doomed? Had the Great Spirit truly thrown them away? If the powers were against them, what good was it to try to live?

Good Hands met him with a look of hope, which faded as she saw his expression. She did not speak but spread his vigil blanket on his bed so as to make it more comfortable and brought him a bowl of broth and a little bread, settling near him to wait till he felt like talking.

He sipped the last taste of broth. His stomach felt better, but his heart did not, and he put off telling his mother about his useless quest.

"How has it been here?" he asked.

Good Hands seemed to shiver. "A niece of Stands Tall died last night."

"The one who laughed a lot? Who was always running?"

"That one."

The lively little girl had always seemed too noisy; it seemed impossible that she was still forever. Walker put down the bowl and stared at the earth, the earth into which his people were sinking like animals in a killing winter.

"There is no help," he told Good Hands. "I fasted, I prayed and smoked and never slept, but I had no vision and got no power."

New Medicine

Good Hands turned her troubled, kind face away for a little while. Then she looked at Walker, and strength came into her voice as she thought out loud. "My son, what is medicine?"

"Why—it is help from the spirits—help to do what you want to do."

"Knowing how? Knowing the way to do something?"

What did she mean? Walker was not much interested in a woman's thoughts just then, not even those of Good Hands. "I suppose that can be medicine, too," he admitted.

Good Hands leaned forward. "My son, you have learned something from your vigil! You know you will not get the kind of medicine power you wanted, the sort we have always been used to. You know that you yourself must find your own help. Maybe that is your medicine."

Walker snorted. "Fine medicine! To know there is none!"

"At least you know where you must start. It is no good to fast and wait on a spirit. You must use the medicine you can make yourself!"

"What medicine?"

"You brought milk for many people. My hen gives eggs." Good Hands looked at him pleadingly and then went on as if afraid of what she was saying, though she was determined to tell him. "Walker! In this place, in this camp, are not eggs and milk more good to our people than Stands Tall's war skill or the old medicine?"

A shadow fell across the entrance. "Do I hear talk of medicine?" called Gray Owl.

Good Hands invited the old chief in and offered him dried plums, which he refused.

Chapter Eight

"I have pain in the stomach," he said. "I am going to the white doctor. Maybe he will give me some of his pills."

"Yesterday you had a headache," Good Hands remembered with a frown of concern. "Did the pills the white doctor gave you make you better?"

Gray Owl peered at her sharply. "My head is good today. I have a lot of the head pills left over. If anyone needs them, I have enough." He patted his medicine bag with satisfaction. "It is good to have all kinds of pills." He turned eagerly to Walker. "How is it with you, my son?"

Sharply reminded of the scarred, wounded horse limping along, trying to live in spite of a running sore that might yet poison him, Walker could hardly bear to look at the old chief.

"There was no medicine, Gray Owl."

Gray Owl sat motionless for a few minutes. Then he got up, moving even more stiffly than usual. "Will you come with me, Walker? I am going to the white doctor now."

Walker, exhausted from two sleepless nights, started to say he was too tired, but something about the old man touched him, and he managed to sound pleased at the visit.

"Yes, I will go. Maybe I can see my red-haired friend and ask if the cows have missed me at milking time."

"Cows!" grumbled Gray Owl. "Milk! A fine thing for a Comanche, the son of a great chief!"

As they went out and passed through the camp, only the women seemed busy. Even the children played with less spirit, and many lay about, ailing and listless. There was a shabby, wornout look to the men, who sat in small

huddles, scarcely speaking, or gathered around dice games or other kinds of gambling.

Comanche, like most Indians, were great gamblers, especially on horse races. It was not unusual for men—or women—to wager everything they owned. Now and then, a man had been known, in desperation, to bet his wife or sister. But losing ponies, tipis, buffalo robes, and other Comanche wealth was one thing out on the free prairie, where a hunt or raid could quickly make a warrior as rich as before. It was another matter, almost deadly, to lose the few possessions remaining to anyone in this camp.

"You cheated!" shouted one man who had led many successful buffalo hunts and war parties.

"You lost!" returned his opponent, tauntingly collecting all the wager sticks.

The first warrior reached for a stone, would have hurled it at the other if their companions had not restrained him. Gray Owl shook his head as he and Walker left the camp.

"This way of life makes sick. It is bad for warriors to have nothing to do."

That was plain. It was customary, of course, for the men to leave the ordinary camp work to the women, enjoying leisure between hunts and warfare or raiding expeditions. It struck Walker with great force that the coming new life, there was nothing for men to do unless they worked for the bluecoats as scouts and hunters. It would be a long time before the whites would trust weapons to their conquered enemies.

"What will happen, Gray Owl?" Walker brooded. "Will the whites try to make us farmers till we die slowly, like the Caddo and Wichita?"

Chapter Eight

"I am too old and tired to see the way. You must find it, Walker. All I can do is beg the white doctor's medicine so that I can give it to people who no longer trust mine."

That is all right for you, thought Walker, as they turned into the hospital. You are old and will not have long to worry about the fate of our people. But I—and the others my age—have long lives in front of us! How can we live them? Begging from white men, living on their scraps?

He was startled from his gloomy thoughts by a groan from Gray Owl, who began to rub his stomach and make faces as if in great pain. Gray Owl would have endured enemy torture or a wound got in warfare with stoic silence, but nothing in the Indian code forbade complaint over ordinary sickness. As Walker stared at Gray Owl, Doctor Miles appeared in the doorway and stood rubbing his beard.

"Sick again, Gray Owl?" he asked in his halting Comanche. "Stomach sick?"

Gray Owl nodded. He rubbed his stomach harder and groaned louder. Doctor Miles held Gray Owl's wrist, feeling the pulse. Then he got Gray Owl to open his mouth and examined the old chief's tongue.

"How is your headache?" Doctor Miles asked.

"Good!" said Gray Owl.

"And the backache you had early this week?"

"Better," decided Gray Owl, giving his spine a gentle rub.

"And your sick ear?"

Gray Owl looked suspicious now but spoke stoutly. "The ear is good. Now it is my stomach!"

"Mmmm." Doctor Miles turned to the big medicine cupboard. He rummaged through the bottles and boxes a few minutes, then turned to Gray Owl with a bottle of large pink pills. The doctor was moving stiffly, and he seemed to be in pain himself, though he grinned as he handed the bottle to Gray Owl. "I think you have a moving-around sickness, Gray Owl. Try these pills. They should be good wherever the pain comes next."

Gray Owl took the bottle. He squinted at the doctor. "You have pain in legs?"

Doctor Miles shrugged. "Just this pesky rheumatism. Can't do anything for it."

"I can," beamed Gray Owl.

Doctor Miles stared. "You *can*? I won't have to eat boiled snakes or toads?"

"No snakes or toads," promised Gray Owl, delighted at this chance to show his skill to a white doctor. "You come?"

"I have to see my other patients. I can't stop till the sun is almost setting."

"Then meet me outside fort," suggested Gray Owl. "Wear old clothes. Bring blanket. I will have cure ready!"

"I will come," said the doctor, but he looked a little anxious. That was fair enough! The Comanche had been afraid of his medicine until they tried it. Some still were.

"You can help me dig the trench," Gray Owl told Walker as they started back to the camp. "Then we will need a lot of sage." He turned his new pills admiringly around in his hand before he stuck them into his medicine bag, looked hopefully at Walker. "Maybe you can get sick, my son, and ask for more white medicine!"

"If I am sick enough to ask for medicine, I shall take it all," said Walker. "But I will ask Duveen to loan a good digging shovel for the trench."

Chapter Eight

While Gray Owl hunted a good place for the trench, Walker sought out the red-haired trooper, who left off drilling men long enough to tell Walker where to find a shovel.

"Be sure you put the shovel back, spalpeen!" said the one-eared trooper, grinning. "And I'll be looking for you at the milking shed tonight for sure!"

Walker found Gray Owl marking the trench between the fort and camp. Under the old medicine man's directions he dug out a trench long enough for the doctor to lie down in. Then, as they gathered sage, Walker told Gray Owl about the horse he had found near Medicine Bluff, about his wound and how he had treated it.

Gray Owl nodded and pondered. "Have you found any thick black stuff running from a hole in the ground?" he asked. "There is lots of it around Medicine Bluff Creek, and it is very good for healing sores. Maybe you can find some for your pony."

"I will go and look," said Walker.

"I can gather the sage," Gray Owl assured him. "After you fix your pony, try to sleep a little, and then be here at sunset to see how I help the white doctor. Someday you may need to know."

Walker had been awake so long he did not think he could ever sleep again. He searched along Medicine Bluff Creek till he found an ooze of thick black liquid that had a pungent smell, scooped some into a piece of bark, and sought out the horse, who had not moved far from where Walker had left him.

"Hua, old warrior," soothed Walker, patting the bony shoulder. "Here is some nice grass for you!" He fed him a handful while easing the mullein plug from the wound.

Then he daubed the sore thoroughly with the black stuff. “If its healing is as strong as its smell, you will be better soon,” Walker told the animal. He brought him more grass, gave him a farewell caress, and went back to camp, where he slept till the sun was low in the sky.

Jumping up, he hurried to meet Gray Owl, who was raking fire from the trench, which was so hot that the ground had cracked.

“Help me line the trench with sage,” instructed Gray Owl, gesturing at the big heap he had collected of that pale green, sharp-smelling herb.

Walker spread the sage thickly. He remembered with a pang that Isatai, the false prophet, had worn a cap of sage stems when he commanded that attack on Adobe Walls where First Son had died. How long ago that seemed! Yet it was only early last summer when the Indians now camped miserably on the flats had made their first Sun Dance and rallied the tribes to overwhelm the white man. It did not seem possible that a people could pass so quickly from hope to despair, from freedom to imprisonment.

Gray Owl poured cold water on the smoking sage as Doctor Miles came up, walking stiffly, carrying a blanket. He wrinkled his nostrils at the fragrant steam.

“Smells like it should do something!” he said.

“Lie down in the trench,” commanded Gray Owl.

After only a second’s hesitation, Doctor Miles obeyed. Gray Owl tucked the blanket around him, capturing the heat and steam. Gradually, Doctor Miles seemed to go limp.

“Feels good,” he sighed. “At least I’ll get a good rest out of it!”

Chapter Eight

"Stay till the earth cools," said Gray Owl. "Then, if pain not much better, you tell me tomorrow and we make another steam bed."

"Thanks," said the doctor, and shut his eyes.

Gray Owl went back to camp, and Walker hurried to the milking shed. Duveen looked up from his cow. "Any luck with your medicine, spalpeen?"

"No."

Walker's throat swelled with remembered disappointment. He settled at once to milking, hiding his face against the cow's warm flank. She seemed to have forgotten him, kept shifting so that Walker spilled more milk than he got in the bucket. After a long silence, Duveen spoke roughly.

"Don't be too downhearted, laddie. White people don't get medicine power, but they manage. You'll have to find your own strength. Maybe that's best anyhow. Nothing can take it away."

Walker murmured something grateful, though he didn't for a minute believe the trooper's words. Who would have believed a bluecoat soldier could be a friend?

"Your people could have a lot more milk if you can find a way to get it to camp," said Duveen. "Mrs. Harris has got a number of her friends to give part of their milk when an Indian can be found who will be in charge of collecting and giving it out."

"I will help," said Walker. "So will my mother."

"That's a start," applauded Duveen, rising as he finished and giving his cow a pat. "Here, I'll fill up your bucket."

He poured the frothing white milk till Walker's pail was as full as he could safely carry it, rested his hand for an instant on Walker's shoulder. "Take heart, spalpeen. You're young, all life is ahead. If you find a way to live in this new time, it will show your people it can be done."

"You are a good man, Duveen," said Walker.

At least he was carrying food back to camp. The milk would send a lot of children to bed that night with full stomachs. But Walker's being cried out in protest as he made his way through the dusk.

He had prayed to bring his people so much more than food, so much more than even medicine power! Most of all, the Indians needed a sign from the Great Spirit that he had not thrown away his red children, that there was hope for them.

There had been no sign. Walker now did not believe that there would ever be.

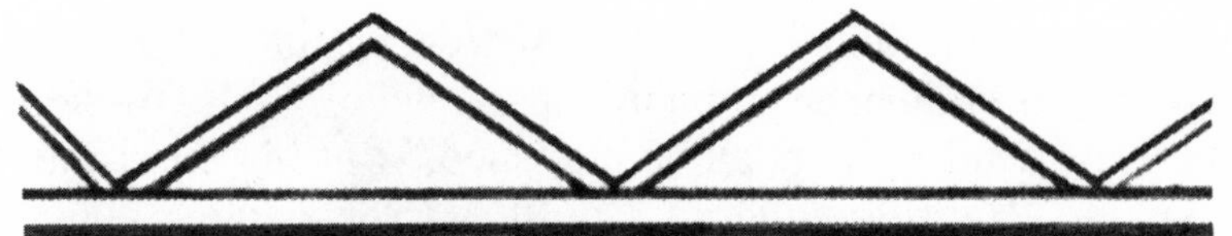

Chapter Nine

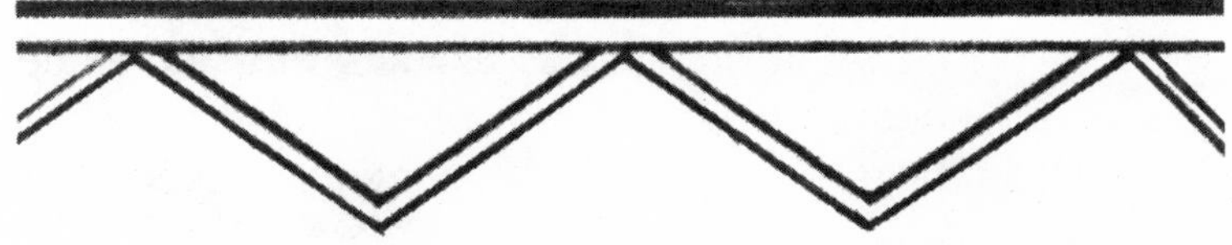

A buffalo had him between its horns and was shaking him back and forth. Even in his dread, Walker was overjoyed that all the buffalo were not gone. He twisted to try to grapple—and woke up.

But he was still being shaken.

"Spalpeen? Duveen clamped a bearlike hug around Walker till he came fully awake and stopped struggling. Good Hands stared from her bed, her face bewildered and frightened in the dim morning light. "Spalpeen," panted Duveen. "Where's the little girl?"

"What girl?" choked Walker.

Duveen whirled toward Good Hands. "Woman, do you know? Little Meadowlark's missing, the child you gave to Mrs. Harris! Have you stolen her back?"

The shocked alarm on Good Hands' face was enough answer. "I'm sorry," the trooper said, scrubbing at his missing ear. "But the child's gone! Mrs. Harris is wild upset, and if I can't bring the tyke back in a few hours, she'll tell the commander."

"And the commander will search all the lodges for an Indian child who is being raised white," said Walker bitterly. "And we may all be punished." But his mind was clicking. He remembered Bright Mirror's anger about the child; worst of all, he remembered how Bright Mirror had said such a girl would be better off dead.

Surely Bright Mirror wouldn't kill little Meadowlark. But he might have stolen her. . . .

It didn't make sense, though, to encumber oneself with a girl child when riding away to roam wild and elude pursuers. Of course Bright Mirror might not have gone. Or he could have left the child with someone, his mother or another woman.

Walker felt a growing anger as he stared at the hunched figure of Good Hands. Everyone knew she had sheltered Meadowlark. She would naturally be suspected if the child vanished. It was not fair of Bright Mirror, if he had done this, to bring trouble on them with his rash doings!

Walker got to his feet. "I have an idea that the child may be in the Kiowa camp," he said. "Must you go with me, or can I try alone?"

Duveen said heavily, "No use causing more trouble than has to be. I'll go tell Mrs. Harris you have a notion. She puts a lot of store by that little gal."

"I will go wait with her," said Good Hands, rising. She must be remembering Bright Mirror's words, too. "Be careful, my son."

"If you can't find the child, troopers will," warned Duveen. "Good luck!"

It was still short of daybreak when Walker found the

Chapter Nine

lodge of Bright Mirror's mother. He listened, heard nothing, and called softly.

There was a sleepy murmur. He stepped inside. Bright Mirror was not there. But in bed with his mother was a child, and as the woman sat up, clutching her robe in fright, Walker saw the little face was Meadowlark's.

So the child lived! At least Bright Mirror had not done anything too desperate to be undone!

"Do not fear," Walker told the woman. "Give me the child. I will take her back to her white mother, and all will be well."

Cradling Meadowlark as if from a thief, Bright Mirror's mother said, "How can an Indian child have a white mother?"

How indeed? It was Walker's doubt exactly. But he said persuasively, "Many a white child has been adopted into an Indian family, grown up among us, and married. You know yourself that most such children do not want to go back to the whites when they have the chance. So if a white can become Indian, why cannot Meadowlark grow up white?"

"Can she change her skin then?"

"No, but—"

"We have not troubled about colors," reminded the woman. "An adopted white was truly one of us—like Quanah Parker's mother." She hugged Meadowlark, who stared at Walker with large bewildered eyes. The child wore Indian clothes again, and Walker had to admit that the hide tunic became the child better than the ruffled garments Mrs. Harris had decked her in. "What can happen to this girl as she grows up?" demanded Bright Mirror's mother. "She can only be a pet, like a pretty animal.

When she is too old to be a pet, what comes?"

"That is a long time away," said Walker. "The Major will look after Meadowlark. This girl would have been left to die if my mother had not saved her. Bright Mirror only stole her to spite the whites."

"He left her with me before he rode off to the plains. He told me to keep her."

"She was not his to give nor yours to keep. The child must go back or there will be great trouble."

The woman only hunched her shoulders over the gift. Full of anger and pity, torn between his feelings as an Indian and his sense of what was right, Walker got heavily to his feet.

"I must go to your chief."

"I will go, too," said the woman. "Kicking Bird has taken the hand of the white man, but there is hope he may say Indians should remain Indians!"

Kicking Bird was a handsome chief in the strength of middle years. Seating his guests in his rich lodge, he listened gravely to Bright Mirror's mother and to Walker. Meadowlark toddled back and forth between the woman and Walker. She trusted them both and seemed not to understand the conflict. Since her real mother's death, she had lived in several homes, been loved in each, and seemed completely happy with whatever adult of whatever color who was in charge.

After he had heard both sides, Kicking Bird turned to Walker. "Do you believe that Mrs. Harris loves the little girl?"

"Yes, great chief."

"And would she want whatever was happiest for the child?"

Chapter Nine

"I think so. But—"

Kicking Bird turned to the Kiowa woman. "And you, is it only to keep the child from the whites that you care for, or do you wish her well-being?"

"Great chief, I wish her well."

"Then, Walker, will you go to Mrs. Harris and ask her if she will let the little girl choose where she will stay?"

"But the whites can take Meadowlark! They do not have to ask! If the girl is not back before noon, a search will start."

Kicking Bird raised a calming hand. "Of course Mrs. Harris can demand the girl. But if she loves her enough to be trusted to look after the child always, then the white woman will abide by what the child shows. We will not ask the girl to choose, Walker. That would be foolish. But both women can be in the room, and we can see which one Meadowlark seems to feel happiest with." The chief said to the Kiowa woman, "If you care for the child, that must seem fair."

"The white woman will offer a toy—or nice food I do not have!"

"Neither will offer anything!" Kicking Bird looked at Walker. "Will you ask Mrs. Harris if she will do this?"

"Even if she consents, where will a test be fair?" asked Walker. "In a tipi Mrs. Harris will seem strange and out of place. But if Meadowlark goes to the house where she has been living for weeks, of course she will cling to the woman who belongs to the house."

"We will meet between the camp and the fort," said Kicking Bird. "There will be neither tipi nor house. It will be fair."

New Medicine

"Then I will go to Mrs. Harris," said Walker. "But do not be surprised if she sends soldiers for the child."

Major Harris was away on patrol, but Doctor Miles and Duveen were with Mrs. Harris. Good Hands seemed most in charge, though, for the scent of one of her herb teas filled the room, and through Duveen she was reassuring the bereaved white woman.

"What is it?" called Doctor Miles, hurrying to let Walker in. "Where is the child?"

Walker explained, and Duveen quickly translated to the beautiful white-haired woman who slowly relaxed as she understood Meadowlark was safe. As Walker went on with Kicking Bird's proposal, Duveen stared and spluttered.

"Hold on, spalpeen! Mrs. Harris doesn't have to go begging for that child! She nursed her out of a killing fever, remember, and has treated her like her own! You just go right back to Kicking Bird and tell him to get that girl here before his whole tribe suffers for it!"

But the white woman touched the trooper's arm, plainly wanting to know the problem. As Duveen, haltingly indignant, told her, she looked stabbed to the heart for a moment and then drew herself up proudly as a chief. She had a strong heart, this woman!

She spoke sharply to Duveen, who argued, but Doctor Miles commanded Duveen to silence and spoke to Walker in his garbled, painful Comanche.

"Walker, Mrs. Harris wants Meadowlark's happiness. She agrees to the test. You go on and tell Kicking Bird we will wait outside the fort."

The sun was not long up when a strange party met in the grassy open space between the post and the camp

on the flats. Good Hands, Doctor Miles, and Duveen had brought Mrs. Harris. Kicking Bird carried little Meadowlark, while Bright Mirror's mother followed. And Walker stood between.

Kicking Bird, with Duveen translating to the white woman, asked the two women to stand in the open space. They could talk to Meadowlark if she came to them and embrace her, but they must not call or coax.

"Then after a little while," concluded the chief, "when she has seen and talked with you both, you must walk away in opposite directions. Do not move to the fort or to the tipis. Do not look back at her or call." He paused. "She will finally go after one woman—and that woman shall be her mother."

He waited till the women had moved off from the others. As he put Meadowlark down, she ran at once, laughing, to her white foster mother, who clasped her in her arms, kissing and petting her. The Kiowa woman stood to one side, her face impassive. But her skin was the copper of the little girl's, and her eyes yearned. Walker felt almost as sorry for her as for the white woman and grew angrier than ever at Bright Mirror for causing this before he rode off to his freedom.

Meadowlark, after much cuddling, caught Mrs. Harris' hand and tugged her toward the Kiowa woman. When she had them close together, she prattled to them both, passing from one to the other, gathering and giving to each a bouquet of grasses.

A very long time seemed to pass before Kicking Bird called his signal.

Each woman gazed at the child, then turned and walked away. Meadowlark, busy with some nutshells, did

not notice for a moment. Then she glanced up, looked from the Indian woman to the white one. She made a soft, startled sound. Then she called.

She called the word for mother in Cheyenne, Kiowa, Comanche, and in the white man's tongue. Neither woman slowed or looked back. The little girl looked at Kicking Bird and at the others.

No one moved or spoke. Walker's chest hurt; he realized that he was holding his breath.

Meadowlark wailed, alone in the space between white and Indian. Then she ran after her white foster mother, who, as the child caught her skirts, whirled and sank down to embrace her.

Kicking Bird went over to give a farewell stroke to the child's gleaming black hair. "She loves her white mother. But I hope she will remember her people as she grows up."

"She will," said Doctor Miles, tugging at his beard, eyes very bright. "Perhaps, Kicking Bird, she will be one of the people who will help the Indians in the new road."

Mrs. Harris straightened, spoke to Duveen, who shrugged and said to Walker, "Mrs. Harris asks if you will tell the Kiowa woman she is sorry Meadowlark cannot stay with them both—and that the Kiowa woman is welcome to visit the child."

Walker went after the drooping mother of Bright Mirror. At first she listened to the message as if she could not believe it. Then her eyes flashed and she laughed scornfully.

"The white squaw has fed the child nice things and given her toys. Of course Meadowlark chose her. I will not see either of them again!"

Chapter Nine

She rushed away, an angry, lonely figure, whose only son had left her to experience this humiliation. Duveen waited for Walker, dropped a rough, friendly hand on his shoulder.

"That Kicking Bird is a wise chief! No Indian can argue Meadowlark was taken by force. But it was brave of Mrs. Harris to take the chance."

"Yes," Walker had to agree.

But it had cut to the heart to watch Meadowlark turn from an Indian woman to run after a white.

Chapter Ten

Little Meadowlark's choosing the whites hurt Walker inside. He did not want to see white people, and he did not like it, the day after Meadowlark's choice, when Good Hands went to help Mrs. Harris.

"Why do you look pleased?" he asked grumpily when Good Hands came in that evening.

"Mrs. Major Harris has promised me a pig," Good Hands announced. "And she is going to ask Doctor Miles if I can work sometimes at the place-to-be-sick-in." Good Hands frowned suddenly. "My son, I saw the doctor hobbling with rheumatism. Why do you not help Gray Owl make a steam bed?"

"If the doctor wants help, why doesn't he ask for it?" demanded Walker.

Good Hands stared at him. Walker grew hot and dropped his gaze. "Maybe," said Good Hands, in a gentle way that stung worse than reproach, "the doctor thinks that after yesterday you may forget that he saved you

once. Maybe he does not want your help if he must beg for it."

Walker could not speak for shame. He went at once to start a trench, and Gray Owl soon joined him.

"Say, this is good of you," the doctor said huskily when Walker went to get him. "And, Walker, to keep me from feeling too lazy, maybe you can teach me more Comanche while I'm steaming. Wouldn't hurt you to learn some English."

So the almost daily steam bed sessions became a kind of language school and a time to talk about both white and Indian medicine.

One day when the steam bed did not seem to have its full effect, Walker turned to Gray Owl.

"Maybe the sweat lodge would help!"

Gray Owl pondered, then nodded.

"Isn't that just for medicine power?" asked the doctor, completely swaddled by the blanket except for his head.

"We use it for sickness, too," explained Gray Owl. "It helps many things."

"Well, I'll try it," volunteered Doctor Miles. His eyes brightened, and he almost sat up in his excitement. "Say, our colonel has bad aches every winter from some old wounds and a poorly healed knee. If you don't mind, I'll invite him into the sweat lodge." The doctor sighed gustily. "Maybe while I've got him shut up like that I can talk some sense into him about keeping the barnyard wastes out of our drinking water! Some of these old cavalry officers swear that it's healthy to keep stable dirt around a fort, but I'm sure it spreads illness. We still have lots to learn about what makes people sick and what

Chapter Ten

keeps them well. In some things, Indians know better than whites."

Walker touched his own properly healed knee. "You know how to straighten bones and do many things we cannot."

"Yes," agreed Doctor Miles. "What we must do is study each other's medicine and make the best of both."

So the colonel and doctor sat in the sweat lodge, and both praised it. The doctor began using the treatment for certain patients, and those who benefited sometimes sent Gray Owl a present. This increased his prestige among the Comanche, so that the old chief was almost content. Walker was glad for this, though he was as downhearted as ever about the future of most of his people and racked his brain for ways to help them during this cruel winter.

In spite of the milk which Walker and Good Hands carried to the camp, it was a season of hunger for the Indians. Now and then a few gaunt cattle were driven to the camp and turned over for slaughter.

Some warriors and boys pretended these miserable beasts were buffalo and tried to hunt them, but it was a foolish game, and soon most Indians were even butchering in the dirty fashion of white people, hacking a beef open so that its entrails spilled into the dirt.

Traditionally, butchering was women's work, but the men did it now as a break in the numbing monotony. Stands Tall was one who slaughtered hastily, squeezing gall on the liver and devouring it all himself without offering even a taste of the delicacy to his wives or friends.

Walker and Gray Owl always butchered together, in the clean Comanche way, slitting the hide, taking off the skin and feet, but leaving the hide under the carcass so

that the flesh could be peeled back on it and stay clean till it was taken out to eat.

Good Hands cooked the stringy beef with chokecherries pounded in to give flavor. This helped, but anyone could tell at first taste that it was not strong and health-making like even the poorest buffalo.

But the buffalo were gone, and people had to eat.

One day when he was visiting the horse, Walker suddenly laughed as he fed him some choice garnering of herbs.

"Your lazy days are over, old one! You are going to haul the milk for me!"

The horse's shoulder was healed now, but though he was always glad to see Walker, he had never tried to follow him into camp. He probably had too good a memory of being beaten by his old master, who had left such scars.

Walker went to the fort and sought out Corporal Timothy Duveen, who scratched his shaggy red hair and said, "A little cart is what you want, spalpeen. The carpenter can stop making coffins long enough to cut us some boards."

Wheels were more of a problem, but an old wagon yielded two. Poles attached the cart to a tongue that could hook to the harness Duveen produced from odds and ends of straps and buckles. It was almost sunset when Walker hurried to the creek with a rawhide halter.

He patted the horse and fed him grass. "I shall call you Medicine," he told him. "Because you are what I got instead of it! And I used medicine to cure you."

The chestnut resignedly accepted the halter and did not fidget when Walker mounted but carried him sedately

Chapter Ten

to the fort and milking shed where the cart waited with two big covered cans.

"I've asked those who will spare milk to put some in those cans when they finish milking," Duveen explained. "Then you can add yours and a bit of mine and take it all at once."

Walker felt pride when he urged Medicine into camp that night. Mothers came to fill gourds and horns for their children, and there was enough for the old people, too.

"I can put eggs in the cart, too," said Good Hands. "Whoever needs them most can have them. You have done a fine thing, my son."

"A fine thing?" Stands Tall pushed through the crowd about the food cart and glared at Walker. "Is it a fine thing to steal a man's horse?"

"I didn't know he was yours," said Walker, shaken. "I found him along the creek. He had a bad wound. If I hadn't got it to heal, he would have died."

"Oh, so now you claim to be a great medicine man!" sneered Stands Tall. "That still does not give you my horse even if he was stolen by the white men." The young warrior started to take the side of the harness to draw the horse away.

Walker got in Stands Tall's way. His heart was beating very fast, but he did not intend to let the animal he had saved go back to Stands Tall's beatings.

"You did not take very good care of the horse, Stands Tall. Still, if you put a price on him, I would try to pay."

"What can you pay?" scoffed the brave.

"I will give you most of my rations for the next two

issues. And I will hunt rabbits for you so your cooking pot will always have meat."

"Rabbits? A little stringy beef, coffee, and flour?" taunted Stands Tall. "No! Give me my horse!"

"You would only beat him to death!"

"A boy does not judge a warrior," blazed Stands Tall, pulling himself erect. "Following your dead brother and old Spring Bull has made you crazy!"

The listeners gasped. It was dangerous as well as insulting to speak the real name of a dead person, especially to a kinsman.

"You call me crazy, yet you speak the name of a dead chief," breathed Walker.

Good Hands came forward. She looked straight at Stands Tall for a long time, till the strong warrior hung his head a bit.

"Mrs. Major Harris has promised me a pig. You may have it, Stands Tall, if you let my son keep the horse."

Stands Tall's mother cried, "A pig would make a wonderful feast!"

Walker could imagine that Stands Tall's mouth was watering; in the confinement of the camp, food was very much on everyone's mind, and Stands Tall behaved like a glutton at every chance.

"I will have the pig," Stands Tall decided.

He stalked away. After they had given out the rest of the milk, Walker and Good Hands went to their tent and unhitched the cart. They left it outside their lodge, but Walker took Medicine down to the good grass by the creek and let him loose there.

"Don't worry, old warrior, you don't have to go back to Stands Tall!" said Walker, patting the chestnut.

Chapter Ten

When he entered the tent, Good Hands brought him a thick stew of jackrabbit and chokecherries and roots. Perhaps she was quick to serve and see to others' comforts because she had never been a favorite wife. Walker felt a surge of understanding and sympathy for his mother, who never complained though life had left her with so little.

"I am sorry you had to give your pig to Stands Tall," Walker said.

"The horse is more important." Good Hands smiled and seemed lighter of heart than he could remember. "A very good thing happened today. The white doctor is going to let me work at the hospital. He wants someone to help with Indian patients, someone who can explain things and tell them they will not be hurt. Gray Owl told him I took good care of sick people, and Mrs. Major Harris told him I had helped her with her housework. So today she took me to talk with the doctor, and tomorrow I will work at the hospital! He will pay me with hens—squaw hens will lay eggs for food or to be hatched. Isn't that good?"

"Very good," nodded Walker. He would still rather have buffalo meat than chicken or eggs or milk, but at least it proved there were other foods. Hard as it was to really believe it, the Indians could live without buffalo.

Winter wore on, the worst season Walker could remember. Every winter the Comanche had to think about food, and it was not unusual to be hungry often in the cold months of scarce game, but it had never been this bad. The Indians lived on what they could get, Army rations issued by the agent and whatever they could hunt.

New Medicine

Misery in camp would have been much worse except for Walker's milk cart and Good Hands' eggs. She took most of her pay in chickens, which she often gave away to other women on their promise not to eat them at once but to keep them as egg providers.

One night as Walker was finishing his bowl of stew, Good Hands sniffed toward the tent flap, set down her bowl, and sniffed again.

"I smell chicken!"

She went to the entrance and peered out, then closed the flap. Her shoulders drooped with discouragement, and her eyes and voice showed anger, which was strange in her.

"The fool woman of Stands Tall has killed the chicken I gave her, and they are eating it!"

"You gave her a hen after Stands Tall took your pig?" Walker asked incredulously.

"Everyone has to eat, my son. But I made her promise not to feed it to that greedy husband of hers but keep it to lay eggs." Good Hands sank down, brooding, as near to weeping as Walker had seen her all that awful winter. "They have filled their stomachs—once—with a hen that would have given them hundreds of eggs!"

"At least he is keeping the pig till it can get fat next year," said Walker. "He is very proud of it."

"What else does he have to boast about?" demanded Good Hands. "He only loafs about the camp or goes off to beg from the Kiowa and comes back grumbling because they have not given him as much as he thinks they should have!"

That was true. Some of the Kiowa who had followed Kicking Bird, the chief who had counseled learning the

Chapter Ten

white man's way, had been peaceably settled on the reservation without loss of their animals or belongings. This caused envy among embittered men like Stands Tall.

"'That Kicking Bird thinks he is a great man," Stands Tall growled after one visit to the Kiowa. "He has a white man's lodge and many ponies and cattle. That is his reward for throwing away his brothers and walking with the white man, but it will not help him long!"

Among the little group of boys and men who heard this was Gray Owl, who looked hard at Stands Tall and spoke quietly. "It would be well for us if we had chiefs like Kicking Bird to help us follow the white road, rather than chiefs who can only dream of war trails we can no longer take."

"At least I do not croak like a tired old bird," jeered Stands Tall. "Your medicine is no good, Gray Owl! You do not believe in it yourself or you would not beg for pills from the white doctor!"

Gray Owl quivered at the insult, but then a gleam showed in his eye, and he gave a laugh of scorn.

"That pig you are so proud of, that pig who is always under everyone's feet, is he an Indian pig then?"

Stands Tall bristled. "He will make a fine feast for those who are still warriors."

The two glared at each other, and Walker was wishing he could think of some way to stop it when Gray Owl's niece ran up.

"Uncle!" she cried. "Come see if you can help my husband. The agent was in our tent, and before we could stop him, he stepped between Red Necklace and the fire!"

It was part of Red Necklace's medicine that no one must come between him and fire. When medicine got broken like that, it usually killed its owner. Walker and some of Red Necklace's friends hurried after Gray Owl, who almost ran to his nephew's lodge.

Red Necklace lay on his bed. He barely looked at Gray Owl. "I shall die, Uncle. The white man stepped between me and the fire and broke my medicine. Now it is killing me."

"Maybe it will not," soothed Gray Owl. "Has your medicine worked in this camp? Maybe it left you when all the Indian medicine seemed to go."

"It has not been able to help me," said Red Necklace. "But it is strong enough to kill me!"

Sweat stood out on his face. He did look as if something within—something mysterious and unseen—were killing him. Gray Owl thought deeply.

"My medicine is not enough for this, nephew, but the white doctor's may be. Let me send for him."

"It will make my medicine angry!" gasped Red Necklace.

"What difference does that make if it is killing you?" Gray Owl turned to Walker. "Will you run for the doctor?"

Walker found the doctor talking to a golden-haired stranger who listened intently as Walker poured out Red Necklace's plight.

"I'll do my best," said Doctor Miles, getting out his bag. "But from what you say, Red Necklace is dying from something that pills won't help." He turned to explain to his guest.

The stranger, whose fair skin gave evidence that he had not spent much time on the prairies, spoke too rapidly for Walker to understand much, pointing to a big

Chapter Ten

black box in the corner. Doctor Miles frowned a moment, then laughed.

"Mr. Wills here has a new very strong medicine. He can catch shadows in the black box which the sun turns into pictures of things. He says maybe if he catches Red Necklace's shadow, his sun medicine can drive away the killing power."

"He can come, and I will ask if Red Necklace will let his shadow be caught," said Walker, feeling cold and worried. It seemed very dangerous to lock the sun in a box with someone's shadow. He didn't want to touch the box, but he carried the rest of the stranger's equipment, and the three of them started for the camp.

Gray Owl came to meet them. He watched the stranger closely as Doctor Miles asked if Red Necklace would try the medicine of the black box.

"I will see," said Gray Owl.

He went into the lodge. Red Necklace's wives could be heard protesting, but Walker almost smiled in relief as he heard the dying warrior's voice.

"The sun cannot hurt my shadow more than I am being hurt anyway. They may catch my shadow and see what they can do."

The stranger gave directions through Doctor Miles. Red Necklace was brought outside and propped up against hides and baggage, while the stranger settled the black box on the long-legged stand Walker had carried and settled a heavy black cloth about his head and shoulders.

"Now my friend, who has very great medicine among the whites, will bring Red Necklace's shadow into the box, and sun power will take away his dying." Doctor

Miles smiled encouragement at the stricken warrior, who breathed in shallow choking gusts. "This medicine has been used on me a dozen times and on hundreds of other people. It cannot hurt you, Red Necklace. And when the sun takes the sickness from your shadow, my friend will give you your shadow, on strong paper, to keep as medicine."

The stranger pulled a cord. A hushed murmur went up from the watching crowd of family and friends as there was a noise and a flash of light.

"It is all right, Red Necklace," said Doctor Miles. "Sleep now, and when you wake, you will be strong and well."

"Do you think he will be?" asked Walker earnestly as he helped carry the stranger's things back to the fort.

Doctor Miles looked at him thoughtfully, dropped a hand on his shoulder. "Walker, lad, it really depends on Red Necklace now and how much he believes in the sun medicine."

Walker froze. "You mean—there is no power in the black box?"

"Yes, there is power, but no magic, no spirit medicine!"

"But power—catching shadows—that must be medicine!"

Doctor Miles drew his heavy eyebrows together. "White men can do many things that are wonderful, but they are done by knowing what will happen when certain things are done a certain way. They can do these things themselves, without what you call medicine."

It sounded like what Good Hands had said—that medicine was knowing what to do.

Chapter Ten

Walker said good-bye to the fair stranger and Doctor Miles. It was time to bring the cart up to the milking shed, so he went slowly back to camp, half dreading to hear the bereaved wails of Red Necklace's wives. All seemed calm, though, as Walker passed near the lodge, and his heart eased a little.

Could it be there was room for the Indian along the white man's road? Part of Walker cried out that his people would be better dead than living like this, cornered on a piece of land granted by the whites. But another part of him cried that life was good and there must be a way for Indians to live.

He caught up his scarred old horse and started for the fort.

Chapter Eleven

Red Necklace rose from his bed next morning, went out, and brought back two rabbits for his family's cook pot. He was proud of being healed by the sun power of the black box, and when the golden-haired stranger gave him a likeness of himself made by the box, Red Necklace showed it to everyone and kept it in a special medicine bag.

It was the only cheering thing that happened as fall settled into winter, a winter as punishing and cruel as the summer had been in its droughts that made game scarce even before the snows.

Food seemed to be all anyone thought of. It was hard on the plains, too, for in February many of the fiercest Kiowa chiefs, who had sworn never to surrender, came into the reservation.

Walker rode over on Medicine to see if Bright Mirror had returned. One of the young braves told him that his friend had gone to stay with the Quohada Comanche, who still ranged on the Staked Plain under the lead of Quanah Parker.

Of all the Comanche bands, only that group clung to freedom. The bluecoats did not want to pursue Quanah on to the vast wind- and stormswept high prairie during the season for heavy snows, but once spring came and the soldiers could start the chase, Quanah would surely be brought to bay.

Walker often thought of the blue-eyed chief who seemed wise as he was brave. Though one of the younger chiefs, he had provided leadership at Adobe Walls after Isatai had been discredited and knew how to draw people with him.

No wonder Bright Mirror had joined him!

Walker longed to. Few days passed that he did not sit astride Medicine, stroking his mane and gazing west. It would be a hard, lonely ride, one that could kill if a blizzard struck, but free Comanche would be at the end of it. When the soldiers came after them next spring, at least some of the young men could fade south and disappear for their lifetimes in the Ghost Mountains, past which the Comanche used to ride on their raids into Mexico.

Yes, high among those mountain meadows, caves, and rock fortresses a few unencumbered warriors could live out their days as free as the golden eagles who made their eyries there.

But every time Walker's heart thrilled to that hope, every time he almost decided to go, he looked back at the camp with its suffering, hopeless people—his people.

He could not go.

As long as he could bring milk for the children and the feeble, as long as he could help Gray Owl, Good

Chapter Eleven

Hands, and Doctor Miles care for the sick, as long as he could make life in the camp a little easier, he knew that he must stay.

But he was glad that Quanah was out. And from the way that Stands Tall and many other braves had turned sour and mean in captivity, Walker believed Quanah and his men might do well to die fighting.

Early in the spring over forty warriors drifted in to surrender, along with many women and children and over seven hundred horses. They had known the soldiers would be after them soon, and the men could not hunt enough to feed all the families whose men were dead or captives.

"The buffalo are gone," these Indians said. "If we live, it must be on beef and rations from the agent."

"Maybe the buffalo are far south," said Red Necklace.

"Maybe they have ranged far north," muttered Gray Owl.

"Maybe they have refuged in the Great Mountains north of the Spanish settlements," suggested another man.

Stands Tall snorted, drawing his blanket around his broad shoulders. "You know well enough where they have gone! Into the earth, whole carcasses rotting, so the white men can have their hides!"

There was silence, uncomfortable, almost despairing. "Buffalo have gone scarce before," reminded Gray Owl. "But the herds always grow again."

"This time the harvest took the seed also," said Stands Tall. "I doubt that on all the plains there are enough buffalo to give one good meal to every Comanche!" He let this gloomy statement go deep and rose to leave, pausing to boast. "My pig is getting fat. When he has lots of meat, I shall make a big feast. Those of you are invited who will, this summer, follow me out on the plains—those of you who will fight the bluecoats and never surrender again!"

He swept away.

"I wonder," mused Gray Owl, "what he will do with his wives and children and old mother?"

"Women and children cannot go on war parties," said Red Necklace. "Even if they did not get hurt, they would be in the way and slow warriors down." He scowled. "I do not want to stay in this camp. I would like to go to Stands Tall's feast and straight to the raiding trail. But I cannot leave my women here, prisoners, to get along however they can."

"You have more cause than most to admire the whites," reminded Gray Owl. "The golden man's sun medicine kept you from dying."

"I would still fight the bluecoats," insisted Red Necklace. "But I cannot leave my family here alone, and there is no place to take them."

Still, talk of Stands Tall's feast came up every time warriors spoke together. They were bedraggled and weary from the prison-camp winter. There were no new good hides to be fashioned into shirts and leggings, and though the women had worked hard to tan cowhide and work it soft, it made stiff, uncomfortable garments, so that nearly all Indians wore at least some articles of castoff or Army issue white man's clothing.

Enough clothes and shelter to stay alive but not be comfortable; enough food to live but not be healthy or

free of hunger. It was no wonder that some of the braves vowed to follow Stands Tall, whatever might happen.

Walker had made up his mind not to go but found himself almost overpoweringly tempted—not to join Stands Tall but to ride toward Quanah and Bright Mirror, far out on the high plains where not even the wind was checked by hills or trees, where the sky settled over you on all sides till you were more aware of it and its sun and moon and stars than you were of the earth. Sometimes he ached to just ease Medicine's reins and keep riding, out along Medicine Bluff Creek and past End of the Mountains onto the climbing plains.

"But there's the milk cart," he would tell his scarred, tough pony. "And I have to dig a steam trench today for Doctor Miles and coax Stands Tall's mother into asking the doctor to help her bad head pains—and I promised Mrs. Harris to get that thorn out of little Meadowlark's foot, and two old men need a sweat lodge—"

So he always turned the chestnut back to camp or the fort.

"You know all my medicine," Gray Owl told him in approving amazement one afternoon while they were making a sage-steam bed for a friend of Duveen's who felt crippled with rheumatism. "You know a lot of Doctor Miles' ways. Perhaps, Walker, you will be a new kind of medicine man among the Indians—one who knows our cures and white treatments, too. That may be what Spring Bull foretold."

Startled, Walker thought about it. He shook his head. "I do not know enough. Sometimes I can tell what a patient needs, but usually Doctor Miles has to decide. White men have schools to study medicine in and learn about all kinds of sicknesses and how to heal, how to cut with sharp tools to take off a poisoned leg or arm or part of even the body, and how to set broken bones so they go straight. I can never go to such a white school."

Gray Owl pondered. "Doctor Miles will teach you all he can," he said with forced cheer. "Anyway, the white medicine schools do not know everything. They did not teach the doctor about the steam trench or sweat lodge. And sometimes even he does not know what is wrong with a sick person."

"That is true. But he tries different cures till something helps—or the patient dies. He says many people are made sick by thinking they are, so he tries to make them think they are well."

"That happens a lot," agreed Gray Owl, smiling a little.

Walker eyed him with sudden suspicion. "Gray Owl! Do all those tiny rocks you show people and say you have drawn out of them to cure their sickness—do those rocks really come out of your medicine bag?"

"Of course they do," said Gray Owl unabashedly. "If the people get well, does it matter? That reminds me that I need some more small pebbles. I gave the last ones to Red Necklace's wife."

"After you pretended to suck them out of her shoulder!"

Gray Owl laughed. "Well, isn't she working again? She will be fine till she gets mad at Red Necklace, and then she will go sick just like she always does."

"That is what Doctor Miles says about some of the white women!" marveled Walker.

Gray Owl nodded, sobering. "Indians and white people are different. But both get sick, both feel pain, both

Chapter Eleven

die—and both pray for healing. Walker! Try to learn white medicine—try to use it for our people!"

Walker turned away. He burned for the strong old power of raids and daring! And Quanah was still free; summer was coming.

One day Walker stopped by the hospital to find Stands Tall berating the doctor. Stands Tall's pig ran loose, foraging, and it seemed it had foraged too widely, rooting up the doctor's potato patch and gorging on the tiny new potatoes. The doctor had shut the pig up in a neighbor's empty pen, and Stands Tall was demanding its immediate release.

"Why have you put my pig in the guardhouse?" he said. "He is a good pig!"

"I am sure he is," said Doctor Miles, pulling his beard in the way he had when covering a laugh. "But he must not ruin the gardens. You must find a way of keeping him home."

"Then he would not get enough to eat," objected Stands Tall. "You should put your potatoes where my pig can't get them."

"And where can't he smell them out?"

"He cannot climb trees. You can put your potatoes up in the branches."

The doctor shook his head. "The potatoes must stay in the ground where they can grow. I am sorry, Stands Tall."

The two men watched each other a few minutes. Stands Tall was very proud of that pig; anyway, the pig was to furnish the feast Stands Tall meant to use to rally warriors who would follow him back on the warpath. Sud-

denly the doctor slapped his knee.

"Listen, Stands Tall! I will trade you a cow for the pig."

"Not regular beef ration?" asked Stands Tall suspiciously.

"No, a free cow, all for you. A farmer gave her to me because I had done a lot of doctoring for his family. She is nice and fat."

"Let me see her," grudged Stands Tall. "I will trade, maybe."

Doctor Miles called an orderly, who took Stands Tall off to inspect the cow. Turning to Walker, Doctor Miles grimaced.

"It's strange to part with a cow in order to shut a pig out of my potatoes!"

"My mother gave him the pig when he tried to claim my horse, Medicine," said Walker. "And my mother has given his wives two squaw hens, and you cured his mother last fall. But Stands Tall wants everything. He is the kind of man who would not get many braves to follow him on a raid because he keeps more than his share of the loot."

"Well," shrugged the doctor, "there are plenty of white men like that, too."

When Walker got back to camp, Stands Tall was already there with the cow, waiting impatiently by Good Hands' lodge.

"Let me use my horse," the warrior said.

"He is my horse. Why do you want him?"

Stands Tall waved a hand at the cow, who stood placidly chewing her cud. "I want to hunt her."

Walker gaped, stared at the peaceful cow, and turned

in disbelief to this man who had once been among the most promising young leaders.

"Stands Tall, you would *hunt* a cow? She is not wild like a buffalo or even those longhorn cattle in Texas. She is a farmer's cow!"

"I am going to hunt her anyway! She will make the feast for warriors, so I shall kill her as if she were a buffalo."

It seemed utter madness to Walker, both ridiculous and pitiful for the cow and the warrior.

"Make your feast," urged Walker. "But do not chase and hunt this cow. She is not made for running, and you will look silly. People will laugh."

If there was one thing no warrior could endure, it was being laughed at or scorned by other Comanche.

Stands Tall's face hardened as if carved from stone. "People will not laugh. Men who are still real Comanche will feast with me on this cow. Women, children, and cowards cannot smile at me behind their faces because the warriors are with me!"

"Whatever I am, I will not loan Medicine to you for this hunt," said Walker. He went into the lodge. After a few stunned seconds at being turned away by a boy, Stands Tall moved off. Walker flung himself down on his couch as the hoofs crunched away after the man's almost noiseless step.

"Hunting a cow from horseback!" Walker said to his mother. "Stands Tall is sick in the head!"

"He is sick in the heart, too," reminded Good Hands. "He and those like him get mean shut up like this without raids or lots of hunting. They cannot change, they can only die."

Hopelessly, Walker said, "Maybe that is all any Comanche can do!"

"No, Walker. At least the very young can make a different life. Little Meadowlark loves her white mother, Mrs. Harris. There are a few white teachers setting up schools for Indian children so they will know numbers and words in books. We older people must live out our lives as best we can—and some warriors may die rather than change. But you are young, Walker, and you are learning much white medicine. You can help our people."

Walker rubbed his head. He thought of Stands Tall and Bright Mirror, and he thought of little Meadowlark in white people's clothes, growing up without learning Indian ways.

"My mother, I do not know what to do! I do not want our people to die—but is it better to end as Comanche, free on the plains, or copy the white man and forget we are Indians?"

"Perhaps we can learn how to live with white men and still be Comanche," said Good Hands gently. "Will you come with me now, Walker, and help me plant potatoes and corn?"

Once she would not have asked him; once he would have been insulted. But since there was little hunting, surely a man must help get food in whatever ways were left. Walker took a bag of seed corn and went with Good Hands to the small plot she had scratched out just beyond the camp.

Comanche seldom grew crops, preferring to trade with the settled tribes like the Wichita and Caddo for corn. But Good Hands knew when to plant what Mrs. Major Harris had given her.

Chapter Eleven

"Put a piece of potato in each hill," Good Hands instructed. "See, there is an eye in each bit, and that will start a new plant."

"Does it matter when things are planted?" Walker asked.

"Yes, we are planting the corn when the moon is full because it grows above ground, and the oak leaves are the size of a squirrel's foot. Potatoes should be planted when the elm buds are swelling."

They worked hard till everything was planted. Walker dusted off his hands in satisfaction, stretched his aching back muscles. "Fresh corn is very good. It will be nice to have our own."

"That is what I hope every family will soon decide," smiled Good Hands. "We had to move to follow the buffalo. Now we do not have to move, so we should grow food where we are." She shivered. "We must never have another winter as hungry as this last one."

A lot of noise was coming from the other side of the camp, shouting and cheering. What could it be? Walker and Good Hands exchanged glances and hurried toward the crowd.

Chapter Twelve

Everyone in camp seemed gathered by the clearing at the end of the lodges. Walker got around to one side and froze, not wishing to believe his eyes.

Stands Tall had painted as if for battle and borrowed someone's horse. He sat haughtily astride, holding a lance he must have fashioned during the winter, while a friend led the haltered cow some distance into the long clearing.

At a whoop from Stands Tall, the friend slipped the halter off the cow. Stands Tall shouted, kicked his mount, and rode furiously toward the bewildered cow, who moved clumsily to one side as Stands Tall thundered past the first time.

Some of the watching people cheered, but many were silent and looked troubled. To put on war paint to chase and kill a tame cow—

Stands Tall crowded the animal. She dodged and turned, bawling, till he pricked her with the lance; then she veered sharply and ran, her bony haunches thrusting jerkily up and down.

Stands Tall circled her, whooping. The cow stopped, heaving. Stands Tall rode in close, tried to prod her into motion, but she just stood, backing a little, till Stands Tall lost patience, rode straight at her, and drove in his lance.

The cow, in her agony, whirled at an angle. Stands Tall, still holding the embedded lance, was dragged off his horse, fell as the cow staggered and collapsed on his leg. He gave a scream and went limp.

Walker was one of the first to reach him, drag the dead cow off. Stands Tall's knee was pinned one way and his ankle the other. This often happened in buffalo hunts, and when it was this bad, the ankle would heal all sorts of tortured ways, crippling the man for life.

"Do not move him," Walker said. "Let me get Doctor Miles."

Doctor Miles left a woman complaining of a headache to come at once. "So the cow was bad luck for Stands Tall! I'm sorry."

"It was the way Stands Tall tried to kill her that was bad luck," said Walker, ashamed for the white man to see that a Comanche had painted in order to lance a cow.

They found Stands Tall groaning, his family wanting to move him, and Gray Owl insisting that he stay quiet till Doctor Miles came. As the white doctor moved through the Indians, Stands Tall sat up, lips peeled back in pain, and spoke between his teeth.

"Why—do you come, white man? To see what your bad-medicine cow has done to me?"

Doctor Miles said calmly, "I have come to see if I

have good medicine to help you." He knelt and would have examined the broken ankle and knee, but Stands Tall raised the stub of his broken, bloodied lance.

"Don't touch me, white man!"

Gray Owl put his body between the doctor and Stands Tall's lance. "Listen, Stands Tall! The doctor can make broken bones go straight again. I cannot. Let him fix your leg."

"No!"

Stands Tall's mother bent over her son. "Remember, Stands Tall, that the white doctor cured me. Let him—"

The warrior glared at her. "If Indian medicine cannot help me, I will die! Get me to my lodge."

His friends carried him home. Gray Owl followed to do what he could. And the wives of Stands Tall butchered the cow, but there was no feast.

A week passed, a week of heavy spirits in the camp in spite of the freshening warmth of spring and the welcome greening of trees and grass. Stands Tall was in fever much of the time. Gray Owl kept trying to soak out the poison that had settled in the blood. He used poultices and some medicines Doctor Miles sent through Walker, but nothing helped. The ankle was swollen till it seemed the skin must burst, and the knee was discolored and had bone splinters thrusting out.

Stands Tall's mother went at last when her son was delirious most of the time, raving of warpaths and big buffalo hunts, and asked Doctor Miles to come.

He did and flinched at the ugly sight and the evil smell that came from the inflamed leg. "The whole thing must be taken off above the knee. Then he might live."

The doctor's voice seemed to shock through the warrior's fever. His eyes opened, flamed with hatred, and he panted, "Get away, white doctor!"

Stands Tall's favorite wife dropped beside him. "Husband, the doctor says you will die unless he takes your leg away."

"My leg? I could not ride—hunt—fight without it!"

"But it is poisoned, there is poison in the leg!"

"Then I will die." Stands Tall gripped his wife's wrist till she moaned. "Don't let that white doctor touch me!"

The women raised their sad gazes slowly to Doctor Miles as Stands Tall slipped back into fevered visions. Gray Owl said, "It is up to a man whether or not he will live with a leg gone. You are good to come, but I think you must heed his wish."

Stands Tall's wives and mother nodded their mournful agreement. The white doctor turned and left.

Another week wore on. In the whole camp, little was thought of besides the dying man. Some thought the white doctor had put bad medicine in the cow to cause the accident. Others said that the powers had been angry because Stands Tall had painted himself as if for war.

There was disquieting news, also, from the Kiowa camp. Some of the Kiowa chiefs and warriors who had stayed out raiding till that spring, when they had finally come into the reservation, were to be sent far away, to Florida, imprisoned at such a distance from their old hunting and raiding grounds that they could not escape. And the burden of selecting those who must go had fallen upon Kicking Bird, the great chief who tried hard to lead his people peacefully along the white man's road.

Again, opinion was divided in the Comanche camp. Some called Kicking Bird a traitor. Others wished that

the Comanche had a chief who could take the white man's hand and bring his people a way to live in these bad days.

Every morning and evening, Walker brought milk for Stands Tall's wives to give him. Except for water and a little broth, the warrior had no nourishment other than the milk.

One night, as Walker helped the women prop up the delirious man so the milk could be poured carefully into his mouth, Stands Tall flung out his arms and knocked his supporters away. He grabbed for the broken lance, which had been left in a corner near him, and, shouting hoarsely, tried to stab it into his favorite wife, who dodged and cowered away.

The other women and Walker tried to catch him, but Stands Tall, in a mighty effort, pulled himself erect for just a second before his mangled leg failed and he fell forward on the lance with all his weight.

They got him back on the couch. One wife ran for Gray Owl while Walker hurried for Doctor Miles. Before either got there, Stands Tall was dead.

"It was better than dying in bed of the poison," said his favorite wife, no longer the giddy young woman who had cooked the hen meant for laying eggs. "He was so afraid of dying like that."

She did not gash her face, though the mother did and the oldest wife. Stands Tall's close friends buried him near Medicine Bluff, with a horse slaughtered on his grave to carry him in the spirit world. His family had bartered all their pitiful belongings for the animal.

Two of the prettier, younger women moved in as wives of sisters' husbands. Good Hands gave chickens to the gashed women, the mother, and older wife and helped them start gardens. Walker saw they had milk. But the sight of Stands Tall's suffering and death hung on him, pressing down his heart, for it seemed the way that many of the strong young warriors, trained solely to war and hunting, must die.

Kicking Bird had made his selection of prisoners to go to Florida, among them the great owl prophet, Maman-ti, and Lone Wolf, who had led a raid to Texas, though Kicking Bird had tried to bring them to the reservation. The prisoners had been shut in the old icehouse where the most warlike chiefs had been locked last fall until it was thought safe to release them. On the day the prisoners were to leave, Walker was drawn against his will toward where the wagons waited to carry away the chained, downcast Indians.

A murmur ran through the onlookers as the proud warriors and chiefs were led out, manacled, and Kicking Bird rode up on a beautiful gray horse, the gift of a white soldier.

He spoke gently to the prisoners, saying that he was sorry that they had to be punished but promising to work for their release and that he hoped they would soon be back to live happily and in peace.

The men looked at him with bitterness, and Maman-ti said grimly, "You are free, Kicking Bird, and have power through the whites, but that will not help you. I shall see that you die soon."

Kicking Bird did not answer. The wagons with the prisoners pulled away.

A few days later, Kicking Bird suddenly fell ill. The agent and Doctor Miles went to him, but he died that

Chapter Twelve

night, saying that he was not sorry to have taken the white man's hand and that he hoped his people would continue in the good path.

Kicking Bird was buried in the Fort Sill cemetery in a huge coffin that held his carbine, war shield, bow and arrows, some money, and a pair of silver-mounted pistols. His horses were killed, and his other private belongings were broken and buried. There was wailing throughout the Kiowa camp, and talk was strong that Maman-ti had made medicine to kill the young hopegiving chief.

It seemed to Walker the Indians were fated to perish. Those who would not change must die like Stands Tall, and those who tried the white man's path would be killed like Kicking Bird through jealousy and resentment.

Brooding, Walker went about his ordinary tasks, unable to respond to Duveen's jokes or, later, to the corporal's worried questions.

"You seem a bit off your feed," concluded the red-haired trooper. "Try not to grieve about Kicking Bird, spalpeen. Keep busy and you'll forget."

But Walker could not. A great sick weariness filled him. He had milked cows for months now, helped feed the people, and he had learned all he could of the white man's medicine. Doctor Miles had even shown him how to set certain broken bones since Stands Tall's disaster so that Walker might act if another Indian should break a limb and refuse the white doctor.

In Walker's discouragement, these things did not seem very important. What was the use of bringing a little food to people who seemed doomed to perish like penned wild animals? What good was it to set the broken leg of a man who had no horse to ride or mend the arm of one who would never throw another buffalo spear?

New Medicine

The Great Spirit had thrown his Indian children away. The old medicine was gone, and there was no new power.

Walker stayed away from the hospital after Kicking Bird's death and gave no explanation to Good Hands when she said that Doctor Miles had asked about him. The only time he felt any kind of peace was when he rode Medicine along the creek evenings and then dismounted to look far away to the prairies.

Buffalo grass bent yellow and rose from the wind, and leaves clothed and softened gray branches of cottonwoods and red-brown boughs of scrub oak and swayed gracefully from willows. Surely there must be a few buffalo out there, just as there were a few free Indians! He was sick of the camp, sick of watching his people go down. He could do nothing to help them, really. He might as well ride on, keep going, till he found Bright Mirror and Quanah's band. Walker understood all too well why Bright Mirror had taken Meadowlark to his mother. They could be friends again.

Always, something made Walker go back to his people in the camp. Yet next day he would be by the creek again, gazing toward the west, longing to ride that way.

One afternoon he heard footsteps and turned to see Doctor Miles coming toward him, puffing a little.

"So here you are, Walker!" Doctor Miles sat down on a fallen log and pulled at his beard. After a while he said, "The Quohadas must come in, Walker. Otherwise they will be followed by many soldiers till they are all killed. I wish that you would go with the party that is taking the Quohadas that message, help persuade them to surrender."

Chapter Twelve

Walker laughed harshly, gestured towards the camp. "I am to tell them to come live like that?"

"If they stay on the plains, they will lose their lives."

"Maybe that would be better! Many have died here, many more must die. I am not sure that Indians can walk the white man's road. I am not sure that Quanah and his people would not do well to die free out on the high plains rather than come here to sicken like mange-ridden, toothless coyotes!"

The doctor stroked his moustache a long time. Then he said, "Well, Walker, perhaps that is what you should tell the Quohadas. You must tell them what you believe."

"Right now I would tell Bright Mirror he was right to leave the reservation! And I would say to Quanah, 'Stay out! There is no hope for our people, no new medicine—only filth, hunger, and sick or shameful death!' "

The doctor winced but his voice was even. "Say what you think is true, Walker. But go with the peace party. Duveen is going. Once he wanted to kill every Comanche, but now, mainly because of you and Good Hands, he wants to convince them they should come in—and live."

Walker stood up. He patted Medicine, stroked his shoulder, still deeply scarred from the white soldiers' massacre of horses. "I will go with Duveen and the party. But I shall tell the Quohada what I think and how it is here!"

"Fair enough," said the doctor, rising heavily. "Be ready in the morning, then. Meet Duveen and the others at the stables. Don't worry about the milking—Corporal Tim is getting friends to see to it."

"How did he know I would go?" demanded Walker.

For the first time that afternoon, the doctor grinned.

He dropped a hand on Walker's arm. "Son, I had no doubt you would go, whatever you felt you had to say!"

He moved off, leaving Walker to reflect that there were only two things he could tell the Quohada, and both were bad: to stay out and be killed, or come in and die slowly.

Fiercely, desperately, Walker closed his eyes and stretched his arms toward Medicine Bluff, the sacred place of his people for generations, inhabited by spirits and once the source of great power.

Help us! he implored. *Tell me something good—something true—to give the Comanche hope!*

He stretched himself between earth and heaven, called with all his being to the Four Directions, to earth and sun; but nothing came.

Chapter Thirteen

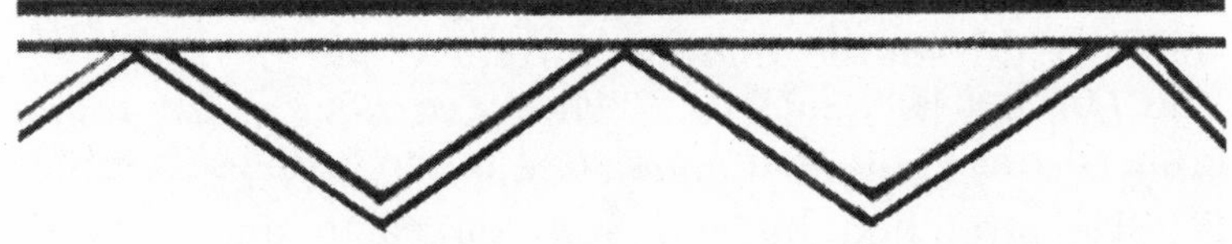

The little group stayed north of the small mountains, following them west through the lush new grass. Walker had often ridden this way, and knew by heart, deep in his heart, all the choices of direction Comanche had once possessed.

Crossing the mountains south, you came to Texas and then to Mexico. Or you could keep on across the high plains, pushing hard between the scarce waterholes, until you came in sight of the great mountains. You could stop anywhere or follow the huge mountains north to the Ute country.

But this time there was only one way to go.

Besides Duveen, there was a white friend of the colonel, Red Necklace, and one of Red Necklace's brothers-in-law.

"The Colonel hopes a small bunch like this can talk better to the Comanche than a troop of soldiers could," said Duveen. He rubbed his missing ear and shot Walker

a grin. "Once I would have been for taking the troop and not talking at all!"

"You are a good man, Duveen," said Walker. "But I am not sure talking is any good. I do not have any good talk."

"Arrah, spalpeen!" roared Duveen. "You're an ungrateful cub! While there's life, there's hope! Nobody ever got anywhere but in a grave by lying down and dying because life didn't go to suit them!"

"We are not like you," said Walker angrily. "We didn't want to get anyplace but where we were! We never crossed the great waters to steal other peoples' hunting grounds!"

"That's the spirit!" laughed Duveen, giving Walker's shoulder an admiring slap that almost knocked him off Medicine. "Never fear, spalpeen! You can hold your own with us and so can most of your people, once they make up their minds that they have to change!"

"How can we change and be Comanche?"

Duveen frowned a minute. Then his bright blue eyes gleamed. "Laddie, haven't you heard stories of long-ago times when your people had no horses?"

Walker thought back, nodded reluctantly. Every Comanche child heard stories of the times when the Comanche had to carry their belongings or put them on travois drawn by dogs. When the horse first came, from the Spaniards, Indians called it the god dog because it was so much bigger and could carry much more. So Walker knew that horses, which were at least as important to the plains Indians as buffalo, had only come to them through white men some generations back.

"And iron and steel," went on Duveen. "You took to using them fast enough, I've even seen arrowheads made

Chapter Thirteen

out of skillets! And show me the Indian who doesn't want a good knife or a carbine!"

"It is true," admitted Walker. "But these things—horses, carbines, steel—all helped us be more of what we were by nature. They helped us move faster and farther, fight and hunt better!"

"That's a quick mind you've got, spalpeen!" grunted Duveen. "Now if you and other bright young fellows would put your wits to seeing what ways of the white man's you could use to help your people, there could be a lot of hope!"

The rest of the group were riding close enough to listen, and Red Necklace asked now, "What ways would help us?"

Duveen shoved back his hat and scratched his flaming hair. Walker could never quite stop thinking what a handsome scalp it would make.

"Well, Red Necklace, the colonel wants to set some of you up as cattle raisers. You ought to see some advantages to raising your meat instead of chasing it, and once you got started good, you'd eat better through the winters than you ever could on the plains."

"I would like to have cattle," said Red Necklace. "But I will never plow the ground like the whites do and cut the grass. The grass is the hair of our mother the earth, and the ground is her body. How can we cut it with steel?"

Duveen shrugged. "Changing won't be easy," he said with rough sympathy. "But it's that or die."

They had left the North Fork of the Red River to travel on the Staked Plain, where water was scarce and there were few landmarks. This was the land Walker had ridden in the old free days and had roamed again with Spring Bull and the blanketed bones of First Son. Not too far from here he had buried them both. Yet their spirits, all the past, haunted Walker, so that this whole journey seemed a bad dream.

Could it really be true that he was riding with white men to persuade the last free Comanche to surrender—or advise them to stay out and face extermination? A year ago they had held the great Sun Dance, the first one for Comanche, and the first gathering of all the tribes. A year ago they had united with Cheyenne, Kiowa, and Apache to sweep the white men off the Indians' hunting grounds, led by the prophet warrior Isatai.

But that hope had died bloodily at Adobe Walls and shamefully in Palo Duro Canyon. In one short year the plains Indians passed from freedom to captivity, from a life of wandering, raiding, and hunting to a forced settling on land marked out by the whites, where raiding was forbidden and hunting, at least of buffalo, impossible.

White men, it seemed, could be doctors or teachers, farmers or traders, cattlemen or magic-makers like the golden-haired catcher of shadows. But for Comanche, every boy grew up trained as a warrior and expecting to seek and receive medicine power, though some used theirs for healing more than as an aid in battle.

Now, except for the few who might become scouts for the bluecoats, there was no use for warriors. And there seemed to be no medicine. There seemed to be no way of life that held any hope. Kicking Bird, who had tried to lead the Kiowa on the white man's road, had been done to death by Maman-ti. This seemed sure, for word had come back from Florida that Maman-ti, the owl

prophet, had told his fellow prisoners that he could use his medicine to kill Kicking Bird but that his medicine would then kill him for causing death to another Kiowa. And Maman-ti had died soon after the captives reached Florida.

That medicine had stayed strong. But if it could only kill other Indians and then bring death to its possessor, what good was it?

Tormented by these thoughts, Walker drifted away from the camp in the evenings to sit alone and gaze up at the stars, which at least could not be put out or driven away by the white men.

Once the plains had seemed as wide and endless as the sky and buffalo as countless as the stars. But on all the five days of this journey they had not seen a single buffalo, here where Walker had often watched vast herds stretching farther than the eye could see. White hunters had killed them.

One night Walker was going back to camp and his blanket when he heard a cry, followed by shouts and confusion. He ran toward the campfire to see Duveen slashing his trouser leg while a big rattlesnake, nearly severed by a hatchet, twitched its last close to the trooper's bedroll.

"It got me right above the ankle!" panted Duveen, sweat standing out on his face. He left Comanche and spoke imploringly to the other white man, who brought out a whiskey flask and then stared helplessly at the stricken trooper.

Walker kept Duveen from taking the flask, remembering something Doctor Miles had believed about that treatment for snakebite.

New Medicine

"Duveen, Doctor Miles says whiskey pumps blood faster and carries poison fast to the heart," Walker said, kneeling and getting out his knife. "Let me use the best Comanche cure."

"Go ahead," grunted Duveen. "I'd rather cut the foot off than die out here!"

He groaned, stiffened, and clenched his teeth as Walker quickly cut out the piece of flesh marked by the snake's fangs and bent to suck out the poison. He spit out the blood and poison, kept up the suction till Red Necklace said, "That ought to be enough, Walker. Here, I have got a prickly pear leaf singed of its spines and split open."

Walker pressed the pulpy inside of the cactus on the wound and bound it in place with a piece of cloth that the colonel's messenger had ripped off the bottom of his shirt.

"Thanks, spalpeen," said Duveen faintly. "Now I'd like that drink!" He took it, and they got him into the bedroll after checking it to be sure no other rattlers had crawled inside to enjoy the warmth. "I was just starting to cover up when that rascal got me," said Duveen. "The rest of you better shake out your blankets in case there was a pair." He squeezed Walker's hand. "Let's hope you're a good doctor, laddie! I'd like to see you again in the morning!"

"We got out the poison very quick," Walker said reassuringly. "I will sleep near you if you need anything."

Duveen chuckled weakly. "Never thought I'd live to be glad to hear a Comanche say that!"

After a thorough look for snakes, the little party settled down. Walker put his blanket close to the trooper. He was surprised at how much he hoped the red-haired sol-

Chapter Thirteen

dier would live—and it had been very good to know the best thing to do to try to save him!

Duveen was restless in the night. Twice Walker gave him water from a canteen and soothed him with a few quiet words. But next morning, though the trooper limped and gritted his teeth while they put on a fresh prickly pear poultice, there was no doubt that he would recover.

"Might as well ride," he insisted when the colonel's envoy suggested they camp a few days. "Jogging along ought to keep the blood healthy."

Duveen seemed feverish, lacked appetite, and was very thirsty, but he did not slow down the party, and on the eighth day of traveling they sighted an encampment on a small river. Most of the people were clustered some distance from the tents, watching two horses.

"A race!" cried Red Necklace and pressed his own horse forward as if intent on seeing the finish. Comanche loved racing and betting on the outcome. Sometimes one band would pool its valuables to bet on one of its horses against the pooled wealth of another group backing its own racer.

This present race was neither won nor lost, for the watching crowd saw the Fort Sill party almost as quickly as it spotted the encampment, and within minutes warriors were mounted and armed, riding toward the messengers.

One of the racers, the rider who had been in the lead on a beautiful spotted pony, turned directly from the race to come with the warriors, and as they neared, Walker recognized his friend Bright Mirror as the leading racer.

It took longer for Bright Mirror to recognize him,

but there could be no doubt when he did, for his mouth curved down contemptuously as he pointed Walker out and said something to one of the warriors.

Walker's heart constricted. He had thought he was over the hurt of his old friend's thinking him a coward and his anger at Bright Mirror's abduction of Meadowlark, but the scorn in the young Kiowa's look stabbed deep.

It is easy for him to be proud, thought Walker. *He spent the fall and winter free even if he did go hungry sometimes. He did not have to worry about children and the sick and old or see Meadowlark choose a white woman over an Indian one or see Stands Tall paint to kill a cow. He did not see his chief, Kicking Bird, name the Florida captives; he probably does not know yet that Kicking Bird is dead, witched by the medicine of another Kiowa. No! Bright Mirror has been living as if nothing had changed.*

The colonel's messenger raised his hand in the sign of peace, but it was a gesture with all the power of the bluecoats and Washington behind it. Walker thought with bitter resignation that Bright Mirror would very shortly learn that the old days were ended, there would not be another year of staying out.

The small group from Fort Sill confronted the scattered force of Quohada. There were several chiefs that Walker knew, Black Horse, Wild Horse—and Isatai! The discredited prophet no longer wore his medicine cap of sage stems and did not speak loud in the short parley.

Blue-eyed Quanah took the lead. "Let us go to camp and talk there," he said. He gave Walker a direct, searching glance. "I know you, son of Spring Bull. I remember your brother who showed such courage at Adobe Walls.

Chapter Thirteen

Have you been all winter at Fort Sill?"

"Yes," said Walker. Somehow being near this strong, forceful young chief who had taken charge of the meeting gave Walker a better feeling, almost a glimmer of hope.

Quanah had been born of a white woman, though he was foremost among the younger chiefs and unmatched in wisdom and bravery. He might be able to help his people find the white man's road in the way that Kicking Bird had led many of the Kiowa. Those strange light eyes pierced Walker.

"I shall want to hear about the camp and how the people fare," said Quanah. "You must tell me everything. But first I will hear the white men and my old comrade, Red Necklace."

As they rode into camp, they passed meat drying on racks. Red Necklace pointed eagerly.

"Buffalo?"

"Yes, we found a small herd and are hunting," said Quanah. "Did you see any buffalo as you came?"

"We saw none," Red Necklace answered despondently. "That meat on your racks is the first buffalo flesh I have seen since last fall."

There was silence except for the horses. Then Quanah spoke cheeringly to Red Necklace. "You can eat plenty of fresh buffalo now. I will tell my wives to make a feast."

Buffalo! Perhaps even a taste of tongue or liver! Walker could almost savor it. But as the older men settled to talk outside Quanah's lodge, Bright Mirror brushed Walker's shoulder.

"Come with me! I want to tell you something!"

Chapter Fourteen

Bright Mirror had grown taller. Otherwise he was the same handsome young brave, his hair parting painted vermilion, and silver ornaments glinting. Walker was hotly aware of his own shabby leggings and crude, stiff cowhide moccasins. It did not help much to remind himself that Kiowa were dandies and loved to make a big show or that Bright Mirror had left his people to face the trouble caused by his taking Meadowlark from Mrs. Harris.

"So you have come with white men to bargain," accused Bright Mirror, leading his sleek pony, which looked as different from scarred, ewe-necked old Medicine as its owner did from Walker. "Well, let us hope that the bluecoats will give you a better horse for your trouble!"

"I did not come for the bluecoats' sake," returned Walker. "And I can say nothing good about the reservation; I told the white doctor I would speak only truth to the Quohada." He added heavily, "The truth is that the

Comanche—all Indians—must come into the reservations or be hunted down and killed."

Bright Mirror lost some of his gay scorn, but his raking gaze said plainer than words what he thought of Walker's condition. "Which is better—to be trapped in the little land white men will allow us or to die out here on the high plains in clean wind?"

"I do not know," said Walker. "I cannot say which is better. I will tell Quanah, and he and the people must decide."

Bright Mirror tossed his head so that the silver disks in his long braids sparkled. "Do you have a white heart, Walker? I am going to find out!"

"What do you mean?"

"Tonight, when the white men sleep, I shall kill them." Bright Mirror laughed. "If you warn them, they will take me prisoner. If you don't tell them, they shall die, and then Quanah cannot surrender. The Quohada would have to stay out and fight!"

"You cannot mean to do this thing!"

The cold smile on the Kiowa's lips said that he could and would. He looked daring, strong, and handsome, all that an Indian should be. It seemed a betrayal of the whole Indian life to do what Walker grimly decided he must.

"I am going to warn Duveen and the colonel's man," he said, turning. He took a few steps, whirled back toward his onetime comrade in a rush of despair. "Bright Mirror, is there no way to change your mind? Do not make me be the cause of your being locked up or sent to Florida!"

"Florida? Have Indians been sent there?"

Walker quickly told all about Maman-ti and Kicking

Bird. Bright Mirror listened as if reluctant to believe, then drew a long shuddering sigh.

"So Kicking Bird is dead," he said of the great Kiowa he had once revered. "That is what he gets for serving the whites!"

"He served his people. It is much better for those who followed him and settled peaceably than it has been for the bands who had to be driven in and treated like prisoners."

Bright Mirror shrugged. "Any man who cannot go when and where he pleases is a prisoner!"

"No man who is responsible for other people can go when and where he pleases," Walker shot back.

They stared at each other. Suddenly Bright Mirror slapped his horse's shoulder and gave a challenging laugh.

"Walker, this is a free Indian pony. Your nag is a captive, just like you! Now if your horse can outrace my wild one, it will prove that being around the whites hasn't ruined him. I will not bother the white messengers, and I will do whatever Quanah decides."

"But my horse has been wounded, and he's old, anyway! A race like that won't prove anything except which horse is faster!"

"It will decide whether you have to turn me in or not," said Bright Mirror. "And it is your only chance of avoiding that unless you want the whites to die."

Walker hesitated. Why should he take part in what was bound to be a humiliating race when he would almost surely have to warn the white men anyway, feel and look a traitor to his friend, who was forcing him into an impossible choice?

But there was the tiny chance that Medicine might

win over the showy younger horse—a slim hope that Walker wouldn't have to tell the whites of Bright Mirror's threat. Walker looked at his old friend.

"I will race you."

"Good!" cried Bright Mirror. "I was beginning to think the camp had drained away your courage!"

Walker fetched Medicine from outside the village. It was really not fair to run a horse who had been traveling hard daily against one which had been in light use, but then nothing about Bright Mirror's challenge was fair!

Most of the men and boys had gone to hear their chiefs parley with the white messengers, but a sprinkling of women and children gathered to watch as Bright Mirror and Walker mounted for their contest.

"Go!" cried Bright Mirror, digging his heels in sharply, setting his horse in motion seconds before Walker could signal Medicine.

Not that it mattered. Medicine stretched his legs gamely, tried with all his might, but few horses, even in their prime, could have given the spotted pony a serious race. He seemed to float, head thrust forward, to the oak tree they had agreed on as the turnaround or halfway mark, while Medicine labored in his dust. Bright Mirror swept past on his way to the finish, hailing Walker with a gay shout of derision.

The next instant his horse stumbled and fell. Bright Mirror's leg was caught beneath his mount. He gave a cry of pain and seemed to go limp.

Walker swung down from Medicine. He urged the spotted pony up and to one side, noting with part of his mind that it had caught its hoof in a gopher hole but seemed not to have broken its leg.

Chapter Fourteen

Bright Mirror had fainted from the hurt, but his eyelids fluttered as Walker bent over him. His right leg was twisted, and as Walker gently explored it, sweat beaded Bright Mirror's face.

"The leg—it must be broken," he panted. "I can't move it!"

Attracted by the commotion, Quanah and his chiefs were coming, along with Duveen and the colonel's man. Quanah knelt to examine the snapped leg, which was swelling at a contused place halfway between knee and foot.

"A bad break," regretted Quanah. "If it mends, it may grow crooked."

The other braves looked gloomy assent.

"Let me try to set it," burst out Walker.

Quanah studied him. "You two were racing. I have heard Bright Mirror sneer at you. Do you want to help him or do you want to make sure he can never walk well again?"

"That's not fair, Chief!" cried Duveen, eyes flashing. "This lad is by way of being a fine doctor! He knows the Indian cures, and he's learning lots of Doctor Miles' tricks. Doc has shown him a little about setting bones." Duveen threw a glance of encouraging challenge to Walker. "I'll help you, spalpeen, if you'll tell me what to do!"

Quanah raised his hand. "It is up to Bright Mirror."

Bright Mirror's face was smeared with dust and sweat. He looked up at Walker for what seemed a long time. At last he spoke in a sighing voice. "Try to help me, Walker. If you cannot, I know it will not be your fault."

His eyes met Walker's in understanding, just as they had before bad feeling came between them over Walker's refusal to leave the reservation. A weight lifted from Walker. Suddenly he felt sure of himself.

"Please, Duveen, will you hold his leg at the knee? Keep it steady as you can while I pull from below."

The trooper bent over Bright Mirror and got a firm grip on the knee. Walker gently, cautiously pulled the other end of the leg, slowly increasing the urgency of his fingers. Bright Mirror smothered a moan but gladly took Quanah's hands to help brace himself as Walker coaxed the broken bone back in place.

When it was done, Bright Mirror fainted. Walker leaned back, limp with exertion. "Now we need to bind the leg straight till it heals," he said.

A squaw brought two strong small limbs and a worn old strouding blanket. She tore the blanket into strips which Walker used to pad the limbs and tie them to brace the leg.

Bright Mirror opened his eyes during the splinting. He touched Walker's arm. "Thank you, my friend. It would have served me right if you had not used your white man's medicine on me."

"A person must use any medicine he knows," said Walker. "I think your leg will be good again."

Walker and Duveen supported Bright Mirror between them to a lodge he shared with his cousin's family. When they stepped back outside, Quanah was waiting.

He said to Duveen, "Will you let me talk alone for a while with this young brave?"

Duveen grinned. "Yes, so long as you don't try to get him to take the warpath! He's needed back at Fort Sill. People depend a lot on him."

Walker felt a little dazed as the trooper limped off.

Chapter Fourteen

Duveen had talked as if he, Walker, were some kind of chief—almost a medicine man! And Quanah had called him a brave. How could that be? The only expedition Walker had ever gone on was that disastrous raid on Adobe Walls.

"Great chief," he said, "I am not a warrior. I have no spirit power. I cannot tell you anything wise!"

Quanah smiled. He led Walker a little distance from the camp, sat down, and motioned for Walker to join him.

"You do not need to give counsel, Walker. Only tell me what is in your heart. Tell me of the winter. Tell me about our people in the camp."

Walker told everything to this blue-eyed half-white, half-Comanche chief; he told of hunger and sickness in the camp on the flats; he told of Meadowlark and Doctor Miles, of how Stands Tall had painted to kill a cow and how Stands Tall had died. He told how Red Necklace had survived his broken medicine and how Kicking Bird had been done to death by other Kiowa. He even told of his horse, Medicine, and the milk cart.

This took a long time, and when Walker was finished, Quanah still sat in thought while Walker scarcely dared breathe for fear of influencing the chief's decision.

It was really a decision for all Comanche. If Quanah brought his people in, it meant he believed they had a chance to make good new ways of life, and he would be a strong leader to find this road.

Quanah raised his eyes to Walker. "Tell me, young man, if I stay out with the Quohada, will you join us?"

Heart thudding, Walker looked over the plains and at the wide dazzling sky. To stay out like this, if only for one summer—his being yearned for it. But the face of

Good Hands rose before him and the outstretched hands of children asking for milk.

"I must go back, great chief, whatever you decide," he said miserably.

Quanah rose.

"I will bring the Quohada in."

"But—I have told you about Stands Tall, about the gambling, how that way of life makes our people sick!"

"And you have shown me that you have learned how to set a broken leg."

"I have told you I got no vision! There is no medicine for us!"

Quanah dropped a hand on Walker's arm. "There is medicine—the kind you have learned, the kind one can do without spirits if one cares enough for our people. So long as some care as much as you do, there is hope for us."

"Great chief, many of our warriors will never learn a different road!"

"Some cannot." Quanah's tone was sad, but as they turned back to the lodges and saw children scrambling and playing, the chief's voice strengthened. "There are many young men like you, though, who can learn good things from the whites, and our children may be happy. I will do all I can to find new ways so that our people may live." Quanah smiled gravely at Walker and moved toward where the council waited.

Ten days later, Walker and the Fort Sill party rode into the post. The colonel's man and Duveen went to report, but Walker stopped at his mother's lodge to show her he was safe and then sought out Doctor Miles.

"So the Quohada will come in as soon as they finish their hunt," mused the doctor, tugging at his beard.

Chapter Fourteen

"You've done a good thing, Walker. You have saved that band."

Walker looked away. His voice caught in his throat. "I—I hope I have not brought them in to sicken and die on the reservation."

"Quanah will put spirit into them. He'll use his mind to solve peace problems now instead of plotting raids and hunts." Doctor Miles picked up a letter from his desk and tapped it. "And I've news I hope will interest you, young one! Would you like to be a doctor?"

"A—doctor?" Walker stammered. "You mean a medicine man like Gray Owl? That is no use. The spirits will not give me power."

"I don't mean that kind of medicine, Walker, though I want you to remember all your Comanche secrets like the steam bed and sweat lodge. No, I've written about you to friends at a doctors' school in the east. They want you to come to them and study."

"At a white doctors' school?" asked Walker, unbelieving. "But I cannot read or write your language. I cannot speak much."

"They will help you. And I will teach you as much as I can this summer." Walker still could not take the prospect in, and Doctor Miles looked disappointed. "You don't have to go, of course. Or maybe you'd rather wait till the big Indian school opens in Pennsylvania. But my friends would start you this fall, if you're willing."

New medicine. A different kind. Maybe Spring Bull had been right.

"And I could come back here—use the new medicine for my people?"

"That would be the whole idea, son."

Walker caught a long breath. Hope stirred in his heart for the first time since Adobe Walls, It would be hard for Indians to take the white man's road, but at least he could help make it a little easier.

"I will go," he told Doctor Miles.

A cheer came from the door, and they turned to see Duveen come in, barely limping. "Good for you, spalpeen! If you can't cure a man with white medicine, you can use the Comanche kind. Doc, you have to get Walker to show you his rattler cure! See this leg—"

But Walker couldn't stay longer, even for praise. He hurried out to tell Gray Owl and Good Hands that soon he would be going away on another medicine quest.

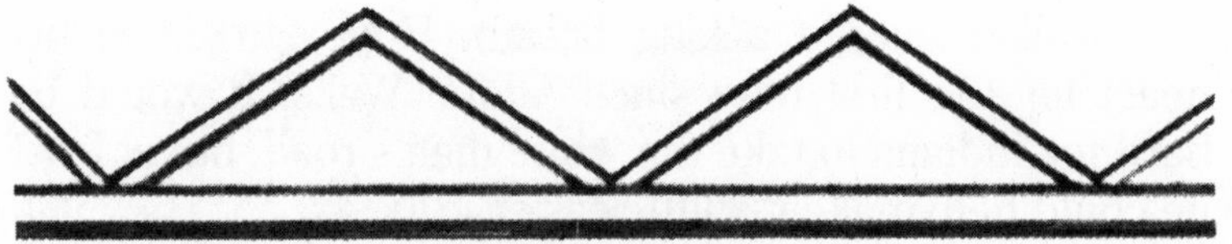

Afterword

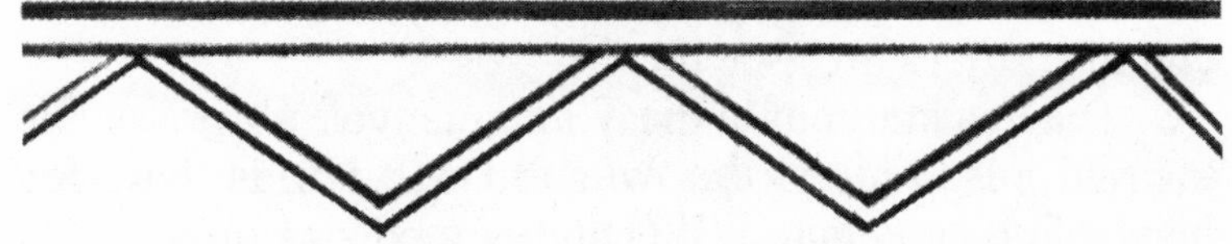

Quanah put his great energy and wisdom into helping his people live in the new times. The year after his surrender, he brought them peyote, which served as an emotional outlet and brought a sense of communion with spirit powers. Peyote is still used in the Native American Church as a valuable part of its ritual. Perhaps because of this and Quanah's leadership, his Comanche stayed aloof from the deceptive lure of the Ghost Dance which swept the plains in the eighteen nineties and culminated in the horrible slaughter at Wounded Knee.

Quanah helped organize the Indian police and sat as a judge, honored by whites and Indians alike. Tragic as the Comanche's story is, without him it would have been much worse. And one must not forget the white men of good faith like Lowrie Tatum, who did all they could to help the Indians survive.

This struggle still continues—the effort to keep the many virtues and strengths of tribal life while living in this century.

The Author

Jeanne Williams has written fifty-six books which have been translated into many languages. There are over ten million copies of her books in print. Her only non-fiction book is the popular *Trails of Tears: American Indians Driven from Their Lands.* Basic to her fiction is well researched history. The American West is a favorite theme.

She is a member of the Texas Institute of Letters and a past president of the Western Writers of America. Jeanne has won four WWA Spur Awards for novels and the Levi Strauss Golden Saddleman, which is given for a lifetime contribution to Western literature.

Jeanne Williams lives in the Chiricahua Mountains of southeastern Arizona, where she is a volunteer emergency medical technician and wildlands firefighter.